THE FINAL
CURE

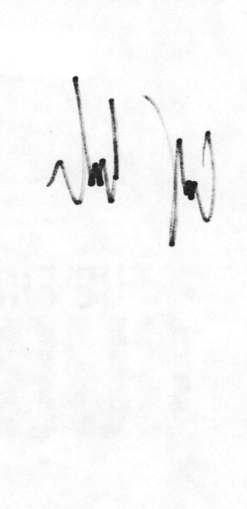

A NOVEL

THE FINAL CURE

CODY THOMAS CHANDLER

TATE PUBLISHING & *Enterprises*

Published by Tate Publishing & Enterprises, LLC
127 E. Trade Center Terrace | Mustang, Oklahoma 73064 USA
1.888.361.9473 | www.tatepublishing.com

Tate Publishing is committed to excellence in the publishing industry. The company reflects the philosophy established by the founders, based on Psalm 68:11,
"The Lord gave the word and great was the company of those who published it."

Book design copyright © 2010 by Tate Publishing, LLC. All rights reserved.
Cover design by Kellie Southerland
Interior design by Nathan Harmony

Published in the United States of America

ISBN: 978-1-61663-489-6
1. Ficton: Science Fiction: General
2. Fiction: Science Fiction: Military
10.06.29

Dedication

To my grandfather and grandmother, for always being there, encouraging my thought, and pushing me to be something more.

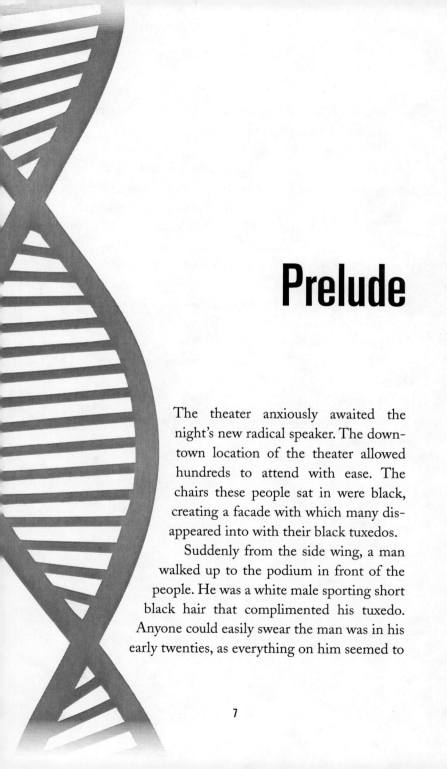

Prelude

The theater anxiously awaited the night's new radical speaker. The downtown location of the theater allowed hundreds to attend with ease. The chairs these people sat in were black, creating a facade with which many disappeared into with their black tuxedos.

Suddenly from the side wing, a man walked up to the podium in front of the people. He was a white male sporting short black hair that complimented his tuxedo. Anyone could easily swear the man was in his early twenties, as everything on him seemed to be perfectly formed, without the sagging or wrinkling of old age. He arranged his notes for a moment before clearing his throat and speaking into the microphone.

"Hello," he stated.

The crowd looked up at him and immediately understood it was time for them to be quiet, while the man fidgeted for a moment before continuing with his speech.

"To begin, I would like to welcome you all here tonight." He paused, building the tension among the masses. "And then I would like to ask how many of you believe in eternal life?"

A few people in the audience shook their heads signaling yes and some signaled no. The man seemed one with the things around him.

"Maybe I should start with the basics, so I don't confuse any of you."

The man paused.

"My name is Laurence Clark, and I am ninety-seven years old."

Cody Thomas Chandler

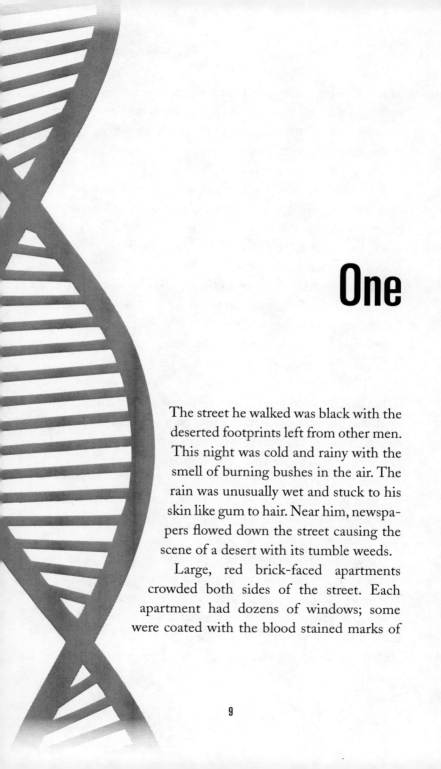

One

The street he walked was black with the deserted footprints left from other men. This night was cold and rainy with the smell of burning bushes in the air. The rain was unusually wet and stuck to his skin like gum to hair. Near him, newspapers flowed down the street causing the scene of a desert with its tumble weeds.

Large, red brick-faced apartments crowded both sides of the street. Each apartment had dozens of windows; some were coated with the blood stained marks of people who contracted the virus. Others were broken with shards of glass sticking out from their corners.

Infection had spread through the blocks of the city like a plague. People were forced to stay indoors, eating and drinking only what they had.

The disease itself ate through the infected people's skin, exposing their insides to other infections and eventually causing permanent blindness. Soon after people lost their sense of stability, while heart failure quickly concluded the disease.

On this night he was out on the streets. He walked not to spread the deadly infection nor to gain it. Nor was he out to defy the government either. No, he walked along to prove what he was, and that was lucky.

On any normal day, this man was very lively, though today he was in all gray raggedy clothes. No life appeared in his face. His walk was a slowed-paced movement. The man had black hair, contrasting his fair complexion. His eyes were a dull blue, and his muscles were fairly formed. He represented a freedom, an independence from the government's constricting hand.

Slowly he turned his gaze to the full moon overhead, wondering what would become of him. In the mist, he watched as a pigeon flew overhead.

A light shown behind the man—slowly sneaking up on the man, it was trying to scare him with its brute force. The light came closer and closer, and the man knew who it was and what it wanted from him. He was out during a continuous twenty-four hour curfew.

The government's wrath would all too soon show itself

Cody Thomas Chandler

to the man, proving his luck had run out for the moment. The lights soon faded into cold, hard machinery. The vehicle pulled along side the man and slowly rolled down the window, mindful of the rain.

There were two men inside. The man walking didn't stop to look at them, but he could see what they looked like without having to turn his head. The driver of the vehicle was a taller Caucasian, with blond hair and brown eyes. However, the passenger was the supposed purer of the two, as he was also Caucasian with blond hair, but had blue eyes.

The driver spoke, "Do you realize you are out during the curfew?"

The man stopped and looked at the driver, who braked to keep with the man. "Yes."

The two men turned to stare at each other for a moment before answering the man.

"We must take you to the base for these crimes."

The man took in a deep breath and responded slowly, "Do as you must." He stood straight up, looking clearly into the rain, awaiting his own personal exile.

The driver put the military vehicle into park and opened the door with the other man. Cautiously the two of them walked to him and placed him into metal handcuffs. These were separated by a solid metal bridge that kept his arms from moving. The man made no attempt to resist, figuring either way he was going to die, so he might as well see what was at the bottom of the rabbit hole.

The two army men packed him in the back, chaining him to his seat, with rough, rusted chains that could be used to contain an elephant. This was his own cold, blackened escape from the surrounding world. He sat and waited until he heard the two doors close, the signal that they were leaving this soul-rotting city. The engine shifted gears and took them off down the last lonely road.

The journey was bumpy and rough while he sat upon the hard seat. His head dripped with rainwater from his outside jaunt with his own demons. He knew that once he arrived to the outside destination, his life was going to change even more rapidly than it had from the infectious life inside the city from which he came.

He glanced out the back of the vehicle and noticed the gates to the city passing behind them. The monstrous structures were thirty-five feet tall and ran all around the community, surrounding all four square miles of the area. This wall was the solution to the spreading disease that threatened the country. This was the end for sure—the only idea the government had to keep the depressed country from breaking into a state of chaos. The gates held in truth and kept out the lies that the government had fed the outer world.

A few moments later, the gates closed and a new object replaced it in view. This was a white, plastic sheet that contained men in masks and white aprons, attempting to block out the chance to catch the disease. In a seconds' notice the vehicle stopped, and the two army men opened the two doors, then shut them. They appeared at the back of the vehicle bed, staring at the man.

The man watched as the two army men lunged effortlessly into the bed and walked cautiously over to him. They released the locks binding him. He was then pushed out the end of the truck, falling to the ground, slamming his head violently upon it. He looked around, squinting from the searing pain. Blood accumulated quickly from his temple.

A group of white-coated individuals surrounded the man. They took him and dragged him to his feet, only to stare at him for a moment.

The man in front looked at the man and spoke, "Take this one to the test facility, and check his blood to make sure he's on the list."

A black bag was then pulled over his face, blocking the world from view.

Two

The black cover slid off his face, blinding him with a large white light. He longed to shield his eyes, but his arms were bound together behind his chair.

They left him sitting in the chair, alone, for over six hours. While he sat, he looked back on what he could remember. After the bag slid over his face, a group of men took him to a room, where they drew his blood with a blunt needle and left him alone in a chair. Soon after, he passed out. From there all he could remember was waking up here.

A figure started to walk in front of the light, a man to be exact. He walked to the center and stood there, hands locked at his front.

"You are Laurence Clark, are you not?"

The light blinded his eyes, and he did not feel the strength to respond.

"Respond or suffer," stated the figure calmly.

The seat grew weary of the man, and the man of the seat. Therefore the man spoke, "I am."

Laurence stood there for a moment before continuing.

"You were found in violation of Marshall Law, more specifically, the twenty-four hour curfew. Do you agree?"

Laurence fumbled on his words for a moment. "Yes."

"The punishment for this is death." A pause was placed in his speech purposefully. "But your country needs you, Laurence. Are you willing to work with us?"

Laurence once again paused, looking to find an answer in his own head, while still seated in his own chair.

"Yes."

Laurence turned and left; the footsteps were the only sounds heard, an echoing of the man's legacy—the only thing anyone would ever recognize him by.

Then the bright light was abruptly shut off, and the man felt his feet pull underneath his chair like he was moving across the floor.

In only a matter of minutes Laurence had moved to the corner of the room. He wasn't quite sure how it had happened, but he knew that he had moved. The room was huge and bare, black and cold. Nothing moved in the room, causing a long, lonely silence.

A door on the side of the room opened suddenly, flooding the room with pure, bright light. Several black figures walked in holding a large, silver crate. The door was then closed and left the room black again. Footsteps and whispers echoed through the area up into seeming apparent rafters above him. Laurence heard clicks and squeaks while the crate was opened, but he had no idea what was inside such an object.

Suddenly a white light appeared behind Laurence, and he was sucked quickly into it. His chair was being pulled violently backward into the light, yet when Laurence turned to see who was yanking his chair to give it the gift of motion, he saw nothing but the white wall. However, before the door he passed through was closed, he noticed that the object the men were unloading was a large pack of dynamite sticks. But why would such a place need to use dynamite in a room that could be used for hundreds of things? Then the door in front of Laurence closed, and his chair spun to face the hallway in front of him.

This sight startled Laurence because he was expecting to find someone tugging him through the hallway. He figured he could have been on a conveyor belt, but when he looked down he saw nothing but the chair moving across the floor, free of any outside force.

Still greatly in awe, Laurence decided that he was going to examine the chair to find the source of its mystery. However, his hands were still handcuffed behind the back of the chair, which made movement hard. The chair was shaped like a pear, except for the fact it had no top, holding his body, constraining his limbs.

Cody Thomas Chandler

Looking down he noticed a bar across his lap and feet, making it nearly impossible to move, even without his arms. The chair itself was made of a strange metal polymer, even one that the educated Laurence had never seen before.

The chair kept moving down the hallway until it came to a dead end about twenty feet from where he started. A mechanical buzz sounded, seeming to report the failure of devices. He sat there staring at the pure white corridor he was seated in. The pureness of the surroundings ate away at his soul. Nothing moved or sounded for some time, allowing his head to swivel around and ache from the silence. Laurence was drifting to sleep, his head bouncing down, when he heard a click.

The chair he sat in sank for a second before abruptly stopping. Laurence snapped back to life and sat still in his chair, his eyes starting to bulge. He immediately understood why the mysterious chair had stopped him.

Three

Laurence found himself sitting in another black room. The chair had fallen straight down through a shaft, rushing him downwards, coming to an abrupt stop. His heart raced from the pure fear and excitement of the fall.

Now he sat calmly straining his eyes to look into the newfound darkness. He could make out a black board and a desk. A bookshelf appeared on his left—filled hundreds of books across—along with a TV on his right, nearly filling up the wall that contained it.

The lights above Laurence flickered, attempting to come to life. Laurence looked up to notice lights. They were unlike anything he had ever seen before; they gave light, yet had a design about them unlike the lights of his community. They glowed blue and were shaped like half circles, hugging the walls.

He was in a room that was rectangular, from what Laurence could tell. But then again there wasn't too much he could see from his chair. The room was a silent black, a sleeping darkness, waiting to be awoken.

A door from the back of the room opened, and a man walked in. He wore all black and even had on black sunglasses. The room came to life at the sound of his footsteps. He walked up to Laurence, put his arm around his shoulder and leaned down to him in the chair. He took a moment to think before speaking.

"Why don't you fear us Laurence Clark?"

Laurence turned his head to face the man before responding.

"It's hard to fear something that you know is a rudimentary lie. Besides, the people shouldn't fear their government. The government should fear their people."

The man stared into Laurence's eyes before coldly responding.

"The government does fear their people, especially when they are sickly and ill."

Laurence watched the man walk around him to the desk. At first, Laurence couldn't believe his eyes. The board in the room wasn't black—it was white. He had never seen anything like it before in his life; its purpose was just as confusing.

"You believe that concealing your fear will help you? Because, Mr. Laurence, you are sadly mistaken. We own the government, and we control the people. There is nowhere you can ever run and hide that we won't find you."

"What do you mean?"

"We see everything, everywhere, all the time. And we get funds by curing diseases in laboratories like this one. In complete essence, we should be thanking your community, Laurence Clark."

"Why?"

"Because you are giving us the most important cure yet—the final cure."

Laurence looked at the man before questioning the situation.

"What do you mean?"

"Your blood is compatible with a cure we have stumbled upon." The man paused for a moment. "To think, you could have been like the rest of the people on the list and died with the rest of those people in the community, and then we never would have had this opportunity."

Laurence looked into the man's eyes, confused and questioning everything. He coldly stared at him with the first slight of anger he had been forced to feel in this place.

"What is the list?"

The man looked at him, laughing at his stupidity.

"The list was a group of people who we engineered the cure for. They were picked, because their DNA was most closely related. And they were the ones who weren't sup-

Cody Thomas Chandler

posed to contract the side effects of the cure—the heart failure, the blindness. However, you were the only one that survived, proving that the deaths of all those people wasn't a total waste…"

Laurence gritted his teeth together as he looked at the man in disgust and vile hatred.

"I can't wait to watch you rot in hell."

The man laughed at the thought of it and walked around Laurence to the back of his chair.

"Don't worry. I'm not a monster. We are just going to test the perfectly formed cure to see how much it can handle. See Laurence, what you have inside of your body is only a piece of the pure power behind this cure. Mr. Conner will analyze you later, but for now you will be placed under confinement."

Laurence snarled.

"Men, take Laurence away."

The man patted Laurence lightly on the shoulder before he walked over to one of the scientists and whispered something in his ear, but Laurence was far too angry to make out the whispers. The man walked to the door before halting and coming back to Laurence, speaking over his shoulder.

"Oh and Laurence, when you no longer serve any purpose, you can expect me to be standing next to you with a gun to your head"

The man walked out, as two men in pure white suits walked in next to Laurence, looking exactly like the men on the surface. They set down a briefcase on the table, opened it, and took out a syringe.

"What are you doing to me?" questioned Laurence as he jerked violently in his chair while the two men looked bleakly at each other.

The first man walked over to Laurence and tied a rubber hose around his arm, pushing his veins out of his skin. The second man walked over to Laurence and paused before taking the liquid from its glass container.

"You're going to wish you were never born. I promise that this will be the end of you."

Laurence looked at his black-coated mask, and sneered at him for a moment before the man stuck the needle into his veins. He pushed down, and Laurence could feel the liquid go into him. It was cold and forced his body to shake and jump. Then he felt his body go into a sudden shock and collapse into his self-contained chair. There was nothing except darkness surrounding him—until he heard a single voice.

"Kid doesn't even have a chance..."

Cody Thomas Chandler

Four

The cell walls were black as night—cold, pure freezing cold. He had no choice but to lie on the floor, as the room was absent of furniture. There was nothing left for Laurence to do but wait in silent agony. The sedative had left him unconscious for hours.

Everything about him felt different. He could see better, even in complete darkness; he could hear farther, even when there was nothing around him, and in turn, he heard things. He could smell things he had never even smelled before. Everything about him was stronger, faster, better. There was no doubt that he had changed, but what would the consequences of these newfound abilities be? Laurence quickly decided it was better not to know.

A slit at the bottom of the door opened, and a tray of food was thrown into the cell. Laurence quickly scrambled over to it, preparing himself for the first bits of food he had eaten in days. After all, food was hard to come by in his city.

The food that laid before him was a nasty mess of water and mashed vitamins. Laurence looked at it cautiously. Then slowly he bent down next to it and devoured the horrid tasting plate of food. Then he crawled to the wall of the cell and sat with his back up against it, allowing his body time to digest the food.

As he sat there, Laurence found there were many intense thoughts in his head, as he had to figure out a solution to the predicament that he had gotten himself into. There was no escape from these people. Nothing he had done in life could have prepared him for what stood on the outside of this very cell.

He sat alone in absolute silence for the longest time, letting his thoughts overtake him. There was a time when Laurence felt a large amount of pain run up through his spinal cord, causing him to curl into the fetal position. He cried ferociously out in pain, for the first time since the virus had attacked his community a month or so ago.

There was a strange feeling inside of him. It made his skin cringe and curl and his body ache and crawl. It made everything about him feel cold and unending. Inside there was a truth that had to be revealed. Laurence felt the lies from before and swore he had nothing left.

Laurence stood up and looked at the door. The walls were semi-reflective, allowing him to see small portions of himself in them. Quickly he looked into the walls and thought, just for a moment, that his eyes turned orange, shining like a cat's. When he blinked, the blue returned, puzzling Laurence's thoughts. There was no doubt about it at this point, this odd and peculiar place had changed him, and now he could tell he was no longer human.

A guard opened the door to Laurence's cell. The man grabbed Laurence by the scruff of his hair, forcefully placing handcuffs on him. There was no speaking, only movement.

The hallway that they walked down was black, stone, and cold. The guard led him straight down the hallway, passing by many groups of cells—all of which contained red Xs on the doors.

They turned down a corridor that ended in double doors. The guard led him up to the double doors, and Laurence noticed that they were sealed by an extensive new metal device so that only a code could open them. From Laurence's perspective, they were the same strange alloy from the chair and extremely thick.

The man entered a code on the side panel. He then opened the door on the left, and led Laurence through carefully, not letting it close by holding it with his back. The hallway was gray and flooded with immense light.

The guard stopped and yanked at the chains binding Laurence. He put a key into the locks and took off the chains vigorously, allowing Laurence to rub his beat red wrists. Laurence turned to look at him, confused.

"You have exactly twenty-seven minutes. Begin."

The guard turned and closed the door behind him, while he waited until he heard them lock on the other side.

The gray hallway stared at him, the doors surely locked, showing there was no exit for Laurence. He stood looking out, finding seven hallways branching off from the main hallway he was located in. Deep in the back of his mind, Laurence immediately understood that they were testing him like a student in a classroom. However, he was still a little hazy on what would happen if he failed to complete the maze.

He stood for a moment, studying the maze, before taking off down the nearest corridor. The hallway twisted and turned, around and around, spinning Laurence up and down. He was forced through tight spaces then out again, twisting back and around. He finally found an end to the corridor, and sprinted toward it with all of his might. Unfortunately for Laurence there was no difference between where he ended and where he had started, except somehow he was certain that he was facing the opposite direction.

Laurence was immersed in perplexity, and turned to his right, running to the next hallway. This hallway had the same effect on Laurence, it took him around and around for several minutes before spitting him back out at where he had started, except on the exact opposite side. Laurence knew in his own infamous intelligence that there were only three hallways left at this point.

Cody Thomas Chandler

He did the same as he did last time; he took a left and went to the next hallway down. From there he ran through the hallway, faster this time, eager to see if the same effect would happen on him. There were several sharp curves this time, along with far steeper hills within the halls themselves. The effort of running ripped away at Laurence; however, he seemed to be stronger than before. The hallway had an ending. This time it spit Laurence back out in the same plain hallway. His newfound theory held true.

Laurence popped out of the hallway, and using all his might, darted to his right, taking the only seemingly different hallway. This one had to lead out of the maze. However, instead of leading him out of the maze, it took him around one long curved hallway that seemed to never end, along with a straight shot that ended in a defeating dead end.

He stopped at the sight of the dead end. Wondering what had happened, he stared at the dead end with disgust. Laurence walked back up the curved corner and stopped for a moment. He looked up and noticed the ceiling was coated with the same metal as the jail cell. Somewhere inside of himself he felt the heat of someone watching him, provoking thought.

He thought quickly to himself, disgust covering his face. Laurence turned around and started sprinting, faster and faster until his legs were bulging with their own might. He wound back down the curve before running into the dipped part of the hallway. The dead end was straight in front of him. He felt the need to beat it down, to rip it from the very face of the Earth.

There was nothing left, no hope, no chance for his survival. These people wanted his life more than anything else, and Laurence wasn't going to try and stick around to find out what happened in twenty-seven minutes. His community was dead, and because of it, there was no reason for his life. But somewhere deep down inside, he found the power of survival reach out and pull him through the fire.

Laurence was running as fast as he could. Then with a startling jump, he leapt into the air, put his shoulder down, and took out the wall that was holding him back from freedom. For a moment, he felt like he had gone through a simple wooden wall, with nearly no studs or supports. Then he opened his eyes, looking at what lay before him. Laurence was falling, falling quickly into a deep hole, a severe pit of certain death.

There was only darkness below him, with the only light coming from the hallway from above. His body felt weightless for a moment, just before hitting the surface below, landing with a thud. Laurence looked up, and for the first time, he knew that the end had to be near.

Cody Thomas Chandler

Five

The blackness above him clouded his thoughts. He could only guess how far he had fallen, which was at least five stories by his estimation, yet nothing happened to him. Laurence seemed to be invincible. He didn't feel like moving, as his body was patiently reconstructing the odds and ends inside of him.

Laurence decided to stand up. Nothing inside of him seemed to require immediate attention. He realized exactly what was happening to him. This cure, this viral infestation of his body, seemed to make him impervious to harm. While he could seemingly still be cut, he was able to repair those cuts in a moments notice. His eyes shone in the dark; he could see things around him that he shouldn't have been able to. The blackness was no longer dark, the light no longer needed.

He twisted himself around to get a clear look at the entire room. This place he had fallen to seemed to be an immense concrete pit with a central column running down into the floor from the ceiling hundreds of feet above him. There was only one exit in front of him that seemed to be the way out of the mess he had gotten himself into.

Laurence rose. While looking down, he noticed a blue stripe that twisted around his arms and body, healing him. This stripe glowed dark and faded as Laurence began to feel better. Wherever it went, his body felt stronger. Laurence quickly reasoned that the stripe was a healing solution to his body.

Whatever it was, Laurence shook it off and continued on his way to the door. He reached out with his left hand and pulled on the door handle. Nothing happened.

Laurence looked around for a second wondering if the joke was on him. However, he felt the urge to beat, to pillage. Therefore, he took the door handle and yanked until the door ripped vertically from its own hinges. The door came tumbling down, falling like a giant being penetrated with an arrow. Laurence stepped away in order to miss the collision.

Inside the hallway was a single door made solely of wood. Laurence turned into the hallway searching both directions for a life form other than his own. Upon the turn, he found nothing, not even a speck of dust was seen in the place. Laurence stepped into the hallway.

His eyes glanced back and forth down the hallway as he walked to the wooden door. Slowly and carefully he opened it, making sure not to damage anything other than what he already had. Laurence felt a wave of curiosity sweep over him as he closed the door behind him.

Darkness enveloped him like a blanket, and it came into every pore, diluting his self-being. Carelessly, Laurence felt the wall for a switch to turn on the lights to show what he was looking at. He found what he was looking for on the left side of the door while his back stayed pressed up against the door.

The lights didn't hesitate to come on, quickly flooding the room with immense light. Inside was a large office of sorts containing a large desk and dozens of bookshelves. The desk was a cluttered mess, and the bookshelves were neatly stacked, except for a single shelf on a single bookshelf. This shelf was cluttered with random books and objects.

Laurence's own curiosity drew him in toward the desk. He didn't know what it was, but it seemed to call out to him. This was the kind of call that made men steal in the past and kill in the future.

Suddenly in the middle of a step, he stopped at the noise of a paper crinkling. His vision snapped to another door on the left side of the room. He peered in at the room, which appeared to be a bathroom, not moving a single bone in his body. He stood there for a moment, not daring to move. Then he peered a tad farther into the room and noticed a fan was blowing air from an air duct into the office.

Laurence relaxed at this, smiling to himself. He took up his walk again and sat down at the desk, flipping through the files that were spread out on the tabletop. They seemed to be on several topics, each in their own manila folder that was also spread across the desk. Laurence found one of interest, as it read "The Maze" across the top.

He took up the folder and sat back in his seat for a moment, flipping through the file before stopping on a drawing. Laurence noticed that this maze was the same he had just come from. The drawing itself was well illustrated and detailed. He could see the paths as they crossed back and forth across a single plain, each corridor he took connecting to another corresponding corridor in a similar hallway. Each main hallway was connected to the other by the curving hallways.

The next part of the schematic Laurence found increasingly intriguing. There was only one hallway that connected to an outer hallway, the very same Laurence was released into the maze from. However, on the other side of the maze stood a hallway that led down into an elevator shaft instead of leading to a dead end. This elevator was labeled "Nuclear Reactor Entrance." Laurence stared at the paper for a moment wondering what a nuclear reactor was before flipping to the next diagram.

On this diagram was a picture of the elevator and the hallways that surrounded the secret car. The elevator itself showed pictures of the explosives on the brakes, and then it showed as the elevator crashed into a nuclear reactor,

Cody Thomas Chandler

destroying everything that existed, including the elevator itself. Laurence shifted his unending gaze toward the other side of the paper, seeing the maze itself.

The ceiling was reflective substance that allowed hundreds of video cameras to watch every angle of the maze all the time. The substance was made especially to be semi-permeable so that neurotoxins, mustard gas in particular, could pass through it with ease. Laurence could sense that these people planned all this in order to keep people away from the reactor, and as an easy way to clean up an unfortunate mess.

Laurence put the folder down, fearing what else he could find on this desk. Quickly he scanned the paper stacks and found what he really wanted. He found it under a stack labeled "Staff." Across the top tab it read, "Estosolo, Arizona."

The folder contained an alphabetical list of the people residing in the town itself. On another page, it had street layouts and town water supplies marked clearly on them as if they were taken from the sky. The detail on each of the pictures was tremendously amazing, far beyond anything Laurence had seen before.

He flipped the page, not realizing the arrogance of the blinding truth. There in front of him stood a map of the water supplies and their deadly effects on the town. Laurence dropped the page on the ground realizing that this base, this very institution, had plagued the town with the Moribund Virus, the town's common name for their so called cure. And then another thought popped into his head. He hadn't died from the Moribund Virus—meaning that whatever it was, it was intended for him and him alone.

Laurence reached back down and picked up the folder. Inside he turned and saw a list of names on a sole sheet of paper. Laurence scrambled down it, searching for the name that he knew would be present. There, in the number seven spot resided his name, among others who Laurence had watched contract the virus and die from it—some of the first to die, if his memory served him well.

On the back of the same page, he noticed a typed page describing the preparation of the cure by a doctor on the base. He used this word "cure" over and over again in the paper, writing about the mysterious wonder of it, and how eventually he could use it to align information with the satellites and other humans. Laurence stared blankly at the page, trying to comprehend things that had not been introduced to him yet.

Slowly, Laurence set the folder back on the table and glanced at the others. One read "Germany" across the top, while another read "Containment." Laurence was fascinated by all of this, and quickly went to pick up the file. He flipped through it, recalling the building of the wall at the first sight of infection. Laurence found it apparent that the government thought this "cure" would be universal; however, they all too quickly saw the whiplash of their errors.

Outside he heard footsteps, such as men marching. Laurence set the folder down and went back to the doorway. He had found everything he needed to know here. Laurence stood there listening for the men to disappear.

Cody Thomas Chandler

Finally, they did, and he sat there for a moment before he decided to move out of the room.

The light switch flicked off at his finger's command, and he stepped outside the sole wooden door. He once again checked both sides of the hallway before heading off toward his right. The hallway he walked in curved into another hallway.

At the turn, he was immediately shocked, as he found a line of guards staring straight at him holding up a defense of Tommy Guns. Laurence froze at first; then he relaxed. The fear of these people was gone. Only the black patron saint of death seemed to love him. A man standing in the center stepped forward, and looked to speak toward Laurence.

"Laurence Clark, come with us."

Laurence looked at the man with calmness.

"Where?"

The man stood there for a moment and looked at Laurence with a defiant stare, as he twitched his upper lip in a fierce manner that made his words come off as sarcasm.

"Men, gather Mr. Clark."

With that, three of the men walked calmly over to Laurence, keeping their weapons pointed at him the entire time. Then smoothly, they surrounded him before, at last, one of them hit him with the butt of his gun, knocking Laurence swiftly to the ground, so he wouldn't put up a fuss when they moved him.

Six

The men dragged Laurence back to his original cell, tossing him inside before locking him inside for observation. He was left unconscious from the blow for quite a decent amount of time, allowing his mind to wander through the day's events.

He was only a tool, and once he was used, he would be tossed away like he had never existed in the first place. Laurence just sat. And there he sat, waiting for twenty endless minutes in emotional silence, while feeling the cold cell walls eat away at his soul.

From several stories above Laurence, a group of men watched his every move through hidden cameras.

There was a scraping at the door as it opened. The light flooded in from the hallway, exposing a military officer in uniform. Laurence noticed that he had gray hair, a scar across his right eye, straight posture, and a pale face. The door was closed behind the man by a guard standing cautiously outside the door. For a moment the officer stood there, looking around the cell before stopping on Laurence.

"Laurence Clark, please come with me."

Laurence hesitated but slowly rose from his seat to walk with the man. Once Laurence reached his side, the man turned abruptly, and marched informally to the door. He knocked once, and the door opened. The man stepped out, allowing adequate following distance for Laurence.

Once Laurence left the room, the guard patiently closed the door. Laurence noticed that the guard was dressed in a formal training uniform for the military—no sleeves or pants, just shorts. He was ridiculously fit in all areas of his body, every muscle bulging, begging for a way out of the area that it was contained in.

The two men walked around several corners to the hallway that the man wanted Laurence in. The hallway itself was vanilla white, except for the hint of purple mixed with blue. While they walked carelessly down the hallway, Laurence twisted around to take in all of the scenery. One side of the hallway held a blue stripe with strange white writing in it and an arrow pointing in the direction they had just come from. On the other side was a purple stripe with the same type of writing in it, only the arrow was pointing in the direction they were headed.

The two of them followed the purple stripe down the hallway until they stared at the ending room before them. The man that had led him here finally spoke as he stopped abruptly at the door. For a moment, he stared deeply into Laurence's eyes, searching curiously.

"Inside you will find a scientist. He will answer any questions you may have."

Laurence squinted at the man, trying to figure what was happening, as he struggled to find the right words.

The man reached for the door and grabbed onto the handle, but before he opened it, he looked back to Laurence.

"You may not understand just yet, but soon everything will make sense."

Then the man turned, opened the door quickly, and pushed Laurence inside. As soon as the door had opened, it was closed again, leaving Laurence standing there alone.

Cody Thomas Chandler

Seven

The room was a deep purple, matching the colored stripe that ran through the hallway. Lab tables dotted the room—each with a black surface that was so clean any given person could see their own reflection in it. There seemed to be no one in the room at first.

However, behind a row of cabinets in the room, there seemed to be some commotion; lab bottles were being knocked together, while someone muttered furiously at them.

Laurence was drawn to these sounds, moving closer and closer to the cabinets, trying to avoid the tables around him. His curiosity took control of him until, stealthily, Laurence came to the cabinets, peering around the corner.

On the other side of the cabinets was another room that was a detailed replica of the other half of the room—lined with the same cabinets and dotted with lab tables. The lab tables on this side of the room, however, were occupied by test tubes, curved glass, and beakers, each with a specific color. To the right was a man, small, black-haired, and pale. His face held a pair glasses while his relaxed check bones made his face seem thin.

The man was fiddling with the objects on the table, clashing test tubes together and muttering to himself every once and again. Laurence crept forward little by little to get a better look at the man. Suddenly, he stopped and turned to Laurence, noticing that he was being watched.

"Ah, Laurence Clark! I've been waiting for you!"

Laurence stepped back from the man for a moment, not sure what to make of this odd man.

"Who are you?"

The scientist looked shocked and then quickly realized he had never met Laurence before.

"I'm sorry for the inconvenience here—um, my name is Condolis Conner. You must have many questions for me."

Laurence stepped around the cabinet wall and faced the man.

"Yes, yes I do…" his voice trailed off. "I don't know where to begin."

The scientist signaled for Laurence to sit in a chair that was stationed under the lab tables in the room.

Cody Thomas Chandler

"Begin wherever you want," stated Mr. Conner as he sat down on a lab stool.

"What is this place?"

Laurence looked at Mr. Conner with interest for his knowledge. Mr. Conner cleared his throat to start his own speech.

"This place is an underground facility built underneath and around the town of Estosolo, Arizona. We design viral weapons while creating vaccinations for some of the worlds various diseases. You, Laurence Clark, are the sole survivor of one of these experiments."

Laurence looked unmoved by this information; he had figured that much out already.

"What exactly am I?"

Mr. Conner looked around searching for an answer.

"You are the willow, and we are the termites that eat you." He paused. "We did not create you, Laurence. We merely used what was already in you and carefully enhanced it."

Laurence stared at the man, intently questioning his ethics.

"What exactly did you change?"

"Little things—like muscle mass and brain capacity for starters. Eventually, we can do even more with your body and others that may become like you, putting them into future versions of the cure."

Laurence became fairly interested in Mr. Conner's words.

"Where did you find this cure?"

"Actually, we stole the cure from Germany."

"Why?"

"If Hitler knew what he had found, we would already be too far behind Germany's army to stop them."

"Where did they find it?"

"The Germans have been experimenting with sending radio waves into space for quite a time now, several months to be exact. However, recently they have been getting responses that are completely comprised of genetic sequences. The cure just so happens to be a response they received from their receivers. Now, we are using their own information to take steps against them."

Laurence rolled his eyes at the thought of aliens rewriting DNA.

"But what does it do?"

"The cure is permanent once it is administered. This cure starts as a single invasive body cell. This cell is similar to a stem cell, meaning it can change into any cell in the body. That cell invades a single body cell and replicates, destroying the original cell in the process. The cells that come from the human cell then attack other types of human cells. However, in the second generation, these cells take the form of the cell they 'infect.' Meanwhile, the original infected cell keeps infecting cells and replicating the cure. The second generation cells then infect one of every type of cell in the human body, never repeating any cell type. This process can only take place if specific genetic markers exist in the human that is infected. In order to contract the cure, all you need is to come in contact with a single cell. This can be as simple as drinking a glass of water—hence how your town was infected.

Cody Thomas Chandler

However, as you've seen first hand, if the cure isn't com-patible with a human, the effects are devastating."

Laurence couldn't believe what he was being told; it was too far off the wall. He sat in silence, waiting to speak. He changed the subject to ease the newfound tension.

"There was a man who told me he wanted to kill me, while I was still stuck in a chair. Who was he?"

"He is General Grimmend. His only concern is him-self and living comfortably. He's the reason they put you in that maze to begin with."

"What do you mean?" asked Laurence.

"The maze does have an entrance and an exit. You were placed on the top floor of the maze. If you could have had more time to explore you may have found the elevator to our power source for this facility, the nuclear reactor. But the point wasn't to let you find the elevator. The point was to kill you."

Laurence looked confused.

"The maze was filled with mustard gas. No one could have survived, but you managed to. Even if you found the elevator, the brake mechanisms would have been destroyed by explosives, sending you to your death in the reactor core. You were only given twenty-seven minutes until they would have let the reactor go critical and melt-down, killing you instantly."

Mr. Conner paused to clear his throat.

"However, you jumped through a wall that led to an empty laboratory that was used to test the first nuclear reactor. And from there you made your way into General Grimmend's office. The rest you know."

"How do you know all of this?" inquired Laurence.

"This facility is lined with cameras and a high speed data transfer system. As things happen, I instantly receive updates from the 'Eye.' This 'Eye' is a room filled with technology that your mind cannot fathom. And there are men whose only job is to analyze data and send it to the employees."

"What kind of place is this?"

"This is a research facility, originally designed to be a genetic testing site. However, this is a government owned facility, and therefore, they placed some of their own specific plans into the facility—things that were too dangerous for the general public to be around."

"If they were too dangerous for the general public, why'd you let Estosolo form above this place?"

"We didn't let the town form above the base. We formed the base under the town. Your community has been used as test subjects for years, testing the effects of radiation, fallout, and now, the cure."

"You're all murderers, you know that?" stated Laurence coldly.

"Laurence, I'm sorry. If I would have known how everything was going to happen, I could've … I would've … "

"Would've what? Sent in a firing squad? Replaced our water with hydrochloric acid?"

The room fell silent for a spell. Laurence looked away in remorse before speaking.

"Why do men insist on playing God?"

Mr. Conner didn't like Laurence's last statement.

"I don't play God, Mr. Clark. I merely do as I am told."

Laurence rolled his eyes at that comment before watching the notorious doctor stare at him coldly.

"Why did you tell me all of this so willingly?"

"Myself and others at this base don't exactly agree with General Grimmend—never have, never will."

Laurence searched the back of his mind for a word, but all he found was an empty pit.

"You are the future, Laurence."

Mr. Conner went to finish his work, but he was too soon interrupted by a door opening on the other side of the cabinets.

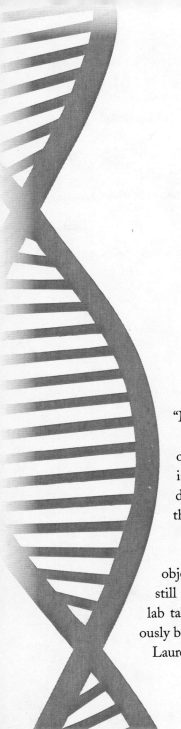

Eight

"Mr. Conner, we must leave immediately."

A voice sounded on the other side of the cabinets. It seemed oddly familiar to Laurence. Mr. Conner himself didn't stop working, yet yelled through the cabinets to the other man.

"What is it, Mr. Shiverson?"

The man seemed to be moving loose objects in the other room. Laurence was still sitting on the stool from beneath the lab table, while Dr. Conner had gone furiously back to his work.

Laurence rose from the stool and peered

through the opening of the cabinets to find that this was the same man that had led Laurence into the room. The man spoke as he was placing several large tables against the door.

"They know what you're doing, Conner. They're coming to kill Laurence."

"Why do they want me dead so badly?" asked Laurence.

"If you ever escape and tell the world what has happened here, we will all be tried and killed. And if anyone else ever got hold of the cure ... well, we'd have a problem on our hands." responded Mr. Shiverson.

Laurence looked at the men cautiously, and then with a sterner face, as he sensed something around him.

"They're coming!"

Mr. Shiverson quickly handed a gun to Laurence as he sprinted past him to the door. Laurence stopped right before the door he entered the lab from and turned around, hurrying back to Mr. Conner. He cautiously whispered into his ear, "Mr. Conner, do you have any acid on hand by chance?"

Mr. Conner looked up with a smirk on his face. He turned and walked around the table and went to one of the many large doors and opened it. Inside he grabbed a large beaker full of hydrochloric acid and gave it to Laurence. Laurence looked at him thankfully.

"Thank you, Mr. Conner."

Laurence took the beaker and quickly made his way back to the door. He looked to the nearest lab table to the door and stood up on it, as he loosened the stopper in the beaker. Then he took the beaker and poured it over the tables and equipment that was lying by the door, making some things fizz and bubble from the instant reaction. He emptied the beaker and then threw the beaker at the door. Laurence jumped down and ran back to the row of cabinets for protection, watching the acid eat meticulously through the wood.

"Finished yet?" asked Laurence as he looked at Mr. Conner who was frantically trying to finish the virus.

"Not quite, this will just take a little longer."

Mr. Conner was cut off by the sound of men at the door, frantically trying to tear through the door. Little did they know of the surprise waiting for them on the other side.

"Damn. Mr. Conner,"—he turned to face Laurence— "there is no more time. We have to get Mr. Clark out of here," stated Mr. Shiverson.

"You have to give me a minute Shiverson. This must be finished."

Laurence and Mr. Shiverson stood their ground at their holdout behind the cabinets—both with a revolving pistol in their hands, cocked and ready to fire.

"Mr. Shiverson, take Laurence to the room while there is still time!"

Laurence looked to Mr. Shiverson and then over to Mr. Conner, still trying to finish his work. Laurence was suddenly cut off by the sound of splintering metal; the men were vigorously coming through the door. The men didn't stop until the door was completely ripped free from the hinges.

There were four of them. They didn't waste any time, running through the door and into the wall of acid. Laurence and Mr. Shiverson watched as it quickly went to work eating through their clothing. These men had their

Cody Thomas Chandler

weapons ready and wasted no time emptying their clips on everything in the room. Stealthily, they tried to take cover behind the tables in the room while reloading, as Laurence and Mr. Shiverson fired back on them.

However, the acid burns prevented the men from staying hidden for more than a few seconds. Their limbs hung out from behind the tables and their heads popped up from the shear pain of the acid eating into their skin. Laurence and Mr. Shiverson fired carefully at their exposed body parts, while the men strategically fired back at Mr. Shiverson and Laurence. Laurence and Mr. Shiverson had the last laugh, though, as they killed each of the men.

Mr. Shiverson looked at the dead bodies sprawled out on the floor and then looked back at Mr. Conner, seeing a terrified look upon his face.

"What is it Mr. Conner?"

"One of the men must have fired a bullet...My work—destroyed." responded Mr. Conner

Mr. Conner looked down to Laurence and Mr. Shiverson as they all watched in horror as liquids oozed and leaked out of several tubes.

"We must take Laurence to the room now, in order to ensure his safety. More men are sure to come," responded Mr. Shiverson carefully.

Mr. Conner took one last look at the monstrosity of ruined work before turning and heading to the unblocked door.

"What will you do about your work, Mr. Conner?" asked Laurence carefully.

Mr. Conner was busy fighting with the door to make it open, but still answered Laurence's question.

"Once you are secure, I will start again and hopefully finish before more soldiers arrive for us. But for now, the only concern is your safety."

Laurence looked around feeling increasingly important. Mr. Conner opened the door using some numbered pad. Mr. Shiverson watched the door cautiously, waiting for another wave of men to enter though the front.

"What will happen to me once I'm secure?"

Mr. Conner took a deep breath before facing Laurence.

"There is something I didn't tell you initially, Laurence. The cure stops aging. Until someone changes your DNA strand again, you will continue to look as you do today."

Laurence stopped, looked shocked, and nodded before breathing carefully to take everything in.

The door led to a back hallway, only a few dozen feet in length. It was pitch black, with long, clear strips for light that slowly warmed up to the men. Laurence was puzzled by the technology around him, but knew there was little time for questions.

There was another similar door at the end of the hallway that seemed to be extraordinarily thick. Laurence wondered what was on the other side of the door. There was a green light and red light surrounding two buttons near the exit. Mr. Shiverson trailed closely behind Laurence and Mr. Conner, watching for people that might appear behind them.

Mr. Conner glanced back at the end of the hallway before touching the red button. Suddenly, the door behind

Cody Thomas Chandler

the men closed, and the room made a hissing sound. Then he pressed the green button, and the door in front of the men opened. Mr. Conner led Laurence inside, revealing a room that had large TV screens everywhere with typewriter-style keyboards and things that looked like lifeless mice. In the center was a large chamber that looked like a bed enclosed in a glass box.

Mr. Shiverson quickly went to work at a keyboard typing away, writing something onto the TV screen above him. Laurence spun around, taking in everything around him.

"Laurence could you please step over here?" Mr. Conner asked him nicely.

Laurence walked over to Mr. Conner.

"Please take off your shoes, socks, shirt, and pants."

Laurence looked at him awkwardly, but did as he was told. Mr. Conner placed little stickers all over Laurence—especially on his thighs and chest, though a few dotted his arms and head. He then continued his work and hooked them to wires that were connected to the curious bed in the center.

"What is all this?" asked Laurence.

"These will monitor you while you sleep," replied Mr. Conner

"Sleep? What do you mean sleep?"

"You must be put to sleep until I can complete my work, therefore protecting you from the men who want you dead. I am truly sorry ... "

"How long will I be asleep?"

Mr. Conner paused and looked up.

"I don't know for sure, Laurence."

Laurence looked around in a state of panic and quickly

found a scapegoat to take his mind from the news he was just given.

"What is he doing?" Laurence asked to Mr. Conner.

"He's fixing the exit."

Laurence looked confused at the unusual statement.

"All your questions will be answered in time, Laurence, but for now, for the safety of you and the research that is contained in you, we must put you to sleep."

Laurence looked at the man, before stepping into the capsule bed. Mr. Conner looked over to Mr. Shiverson and then closed the glass sheet over the bed.

He yelled inside to Laurence, "You will see a pink gas come into the chamber. Try to stay calm. It will relax you and put you into a deep sleep."

Laurence gave him the thumbs up—smiling awkwardly on one side of his face, though, on the inside, he felt anger toward Mr. Conner for bringing his life into such a mess. Then with a bang, the room shook, and Laurence panicked, hitting on the glass and yelling at Mr. Conner. Mr. Conner ran to the tube and yelled, "Remain calm!" before pressing a button that would release the sleeping gas. Suddenly, from his feet came a pink gas that soon filled the entire chamber. Laurence tried not to breathe at first, but then it became inevitable. The gas stung the back of his throat as it went down. He was thinking, trying to keep conscious, but he couldn't.

Laurence was in a world of darkness now; his mind slowly ventured away from 1939, the virus, and the entire complex itself. He was in a deep and unconscious sleep that drifted back to the death of his parents. For a moment,

Laurence felt like he was able to reach out and touch his parents as he watched them scream out in horror at the very thing that only Laurence could control. Pain lined their faces, but soon enough, it was over again as Laurence sailed off into a new world.

Nine

The fog lifted from inside the chamber, revealing the sleeping Laurence Clark. The surrounding room hadn't changed since 1939, and neither had Laurence. Men surrounded the chamber. They typed hurriedly at the computers, shutting off everything that kept Laurence alive for so many years in the cryotube. The glass sheet moved back, and Laurence's eyes flickered. A man stepped forward holding clothes.

"Hello, Laurence Clark. It's good to see

that you are alive after all of these years. When you're ready, put on these clothes."

The man tossed the clothes on Laurence's lap. Then the men went back to the computers, typing frantically away at them.

Laurence's eyes closed, and he went into a dark and restful sleep, as the men around the container went to work trying to figure out what happened with this mysterious man. Laurence's mind cut in and out of reality, and for moments, he could remember the virus, the town, and even the secrets of Mr. Conner.

At last, he awoke. Feeling revived and alive, he opened his eyes and rose from the glass cryo-tube. He looked up to see five men standing around him, each in a pure black jumpsuit with black sunglasses. Laurence looked at the mass of them, unfamiliar with the new appearance of staff personnel. For a second, he couldn't breathe, but he pushed on to find his voice.

"What year is it?"

The men all exchanged glances, yet none spoke. Laurence figured he would ask again.

"What year is it?"

The man on the right side of Laurence, his name tag reading Kaluzny, spoke first.

"The year is 2010. It's July 24, 2010, to be exact."

Laurence looked around and thought about the seventy-one years he had missed in the tube. He noticed that the door that sealed him in the room had been drilled through, with concrete as a secure filler.

"Why was I was sealed in this room?"

A taller, brown-haired man on the right took this question.

"To ensure the survival of the most important thing in genetic experimentation." The man paused. "You were sealed in six feet of concrete in every direction. Looks like someone really wanted to keep you alive."

Laurence glanced around at the men, nervously trying to make conversation with a new culture of people.

"So what's 2010 like?"

Ten

Laurence was now technically ninety-seven years of age, yet no one around him could even tell the difference. Laurence was touching the computers around him, looking at them with an intense curiosity.

"Laurence Clark? Sir, are you going to come out here or not?" asked one of the men.

Laurence turned to look through the tunnel at the room, which had been the beginnings of his renaissance.

"I'll be just a moment."

Laurence continued to look at the computer. He was surprised at the remarkable technology the government had hidden from the people of 1939. He wondered what new technology these people could be hiding in 2010.

He took one last glance around, burning the image into his memory. Then he walked over to the circle in the wall and crawled through to the beaten down laboratory.

The walls that surrounded Laurence, the same walls that used to be covered in cabinets, were now filled with black soot. The laboratory had been destroyed. Laurence figured that it could have occurred during Mr. Conner and Mr. Shiverson's own personal standoff with the general's men.

Where there was once a wall of cabinets separating the two sections of the lab, there was now a hole, about twelve feet in diameter and cut from the surface.

"What happened here?"

Laurence looked around at the men waiting for a response, especially looking at the two holes in the rooms.

"When they put you into cryo-sleep, they sealed the room with a concrete barrier, hiding the entire hallway. We had to cut through it to get you out. Most of this base was destroyed at approximately the same time, according to the computers."

Laurence looked confused. The man shook his head and pointed at a computer monitor. "Computer."

Laurence shook his head as if he understood, while the man continued, "Then the base flooded from a nearby underground spring. The only thing left was this hole leading to the surface. To get down here, we had to drain the entire thing," stated Raymond, the man closest to Laurence.

The men were walking around the lab, some started hooking gear up near the base of the hole. One man pushed a button and light from the surface shown down onto the floor. Raymond spoke again.

"The details are scattered, but as far as we can tell, someone placed bombs in several storage facilities and control rooms, destroying many of the base's mechanical systems and automatic locks. The hallways were flooded with water from the spring. Unfortunately, in the struggle, the entire base was nearly destroyed, minus these two rooms and a few other random closets here and there. We figure these rooms were protected by several feet of concrete and didn't have automatic locks. However, we believe this room flooded because the door was corroded by acid from the inside out."

Laurence gazed at the floor saddened by the thoughts of the past. He took in a deep breath, quietly paying his respects to the men who saved him. Laurence then asked a hopeful question.

"What about the town above the base?"

Laurence watched as the soldiers shuffled their feet.

"The entire thing collapsed into the lake," responded the men quietly. Everyone looked around, trying to figure out what to say next. Finally, the leader of the group spoke up.

"Come over here, Laurence. All your other questions will have answers waiting for you on the surface."

With that, Laurence walked over to the circle of men. He was cautious at first, but relaxed as he waited with the other men who stood around the device that would transport them to the surface. These men formed up while Laurence was being informed on the base's short-lived history.

He glanced man to man waiting for something to pull them up, but as soon as he started to ask them what was happening, a giant water drop like object fell from the sky and stopped about three feet from the ground. It was a giant sphere that was about two, maybe three feet in diameter. The object was silvery, allowing Laurence to see himself in the reflection given off by it.

Suddenly, without warning, the sphere bent out oddly, stretching, reaching, grabbing at the reflections of the men. Then with a sudden jerk, the sphere bent straight out, grabbing around the men and sucking them into itself. Laurence felt an extremely cold shock run up his spine and through his body from the silver water drop, following with a rush of wind before he blacked out.

Laurence finally came to and immediately felt sick. He quickly fumbled to his feet and began to vomit. He leaned over with has hands resting uneasily on his knees, panting. He felt himself bend straight back up and swing about his waist, almost like the motion of a drunken man. He looked around feeling incredibly sick and dizzy.

A man who led him out of the chamber came down and leaned down next to Laurence.

"Don't worry, happens to all of us the first time." Laurence threw up again, turning the man away, but he

Cody Thomas Chandler

still called out with his back turned to him, "You can call me Coverton if you ever need me."

Laurence barely squeaked out a thanks before passing out on the ground.

Laurence awoke quite a spell later. He was lying on a table. He had a runny nose, and his face felt hot; he could barely move. He turned his head to see a single doctor, busy working at his computer. He coughed once to clear his boiling throat. The doctor immediately turned around.

Laurence looked at him, amazed. He looked exactly like Mr. Conner, except younger and stronger. His eyes were a dull green, and his hair was short; everything about him was an improvement over his grandfather.

"Mr. Conner?" asked Laurence.

The man looked up at him intently, laughing a little to himself.

"Yes, that is my name. However, I think you may be speaking of my grandfather. I am Benedict Conner, grandson of the man you once knew, Condolis Conner."

Laurence looked at him like he was crazy.

"But if you want, you can just call me Doc for short."

Laurence looked back at the ceiling before looking down at his hands. "Doc, what's wrong with me?"

"What do you mean?"

"I'm ninety-seven. My hands aren't wrinkled, and I'm pretty sure my face is the same. Your grandfather wasn't kidding when he said I wouldn't age, was he?"

Dr. Conner pulled his chair up to Laurence's bedside.

"Let me tell you something, Laurence." He paused for a moment. "There were many unclear effects of the cure.

The longer the cure sits in your bloodstream, the stronger you will become. You will be able to heal yourself instantaneously. You can regenerate, your muscles are stronger and can grow at exponential rates, and you will no longer age. I'm sorry, but there's really not much I can do."

His voice trailed off, and Laurence looked over at him, concerned.

"Can you change me back? I mean, remove the cure?"

Dr. Conner looked down at Laurence with no remorse.

"There is a solution to the cure. My grandfather came up with a reverse to the cure, called V3, which stands for Version Three. There are hundreds of versions of the cure, each with its own specific side-effects. However, V3 had its own flaws. When injected into a human with the cure, it will slowly take back all of the benefits, until cancer progresses in every crevice of the body and the human dies.

Laurence looked back to the floor.

"So I'm stuck like this?"

"More or less."

Laurence shook his head as a tear fell from his eyes.

"Why did you even wake me up? Why not just let me sleep until I die?"

"We had our reasons, Laurence."

Laurence looked back at him with his spare hope, turning his focus to a vile of blood on the counter and then to the inside of his elbow where he found a bandage.

"Sorry about that," spoke Dr. Conner, "I had to take your blood while you were out, so I could begin my work."

Laurence wondered what else these people could have done to him in his sleep but found himself quick to

Cody Thomas Chandler

trust Dr. Conner because of his relations to the late Mr. Condolis Conner. Dr. Conner turned to his work, taking his attention from Laurence.

"I think you better rest, Laurence. You may need it."

Eleven

Dr. Conner decided while Laurence was asleep that it would be best if Laurence took a tour of the new facility with two guards. They were Coverton, who Laurence was quite familiar with, and Gonzalez, who he barely knew. Coverton was a taller man who was built like a rhinoceros, which offset the skinnier but equally tall Gonzalez. The men had brought Laurence to the outside world, which was comprised mostly of sand. The outside complex was a gigantic facility with several barracks and buildings a few stories tall. They were above, and shifted slightly to the right from the lake, the old underground base and Laurence's former community. There was a lake that had a single runway extending to its center. The landscape surrounding the lake was a barren desert—surely proving Laurence's town was gone.

"What happened to the town that used to be here?"

Coverton was walking along with Laurence and Gonzalez and quickly stepped in to answer.

"It was engulfed by the lake you see there."

"So what exactly does Doc want me to see out here?" asked Laurence as they walked toward a row of sheds that lined a poorly constructed road. These sheds were each labeled with various letters and numbers. Then the men stopped and opened the door to a shed.

Inside, Laurence saw dozens of weapons lined up on shelving that surrounded every wall in the shed. His eyes lit up with the purity of dark excitement.

"Welcome to Weapons Shed Number Two," stated Gonzalez. "Everything that has been approved for use on this base you can find here. Anything that has not yet been approved for use is located in Weapons Shed Number Eight, also known as the Experimental Weapons Shed."

Laurence walked inside and touched one of the handles of the weapons.

"You like?" asked Richardson.

Laurence just walked along, touching each handle.

"Maybe if we have time later we can test some of these weapons out. But for now we need to keep moving."

Laurence walked out of the shed and watched as

Coverton locked the shed again. Then Laurence was led down the road as the sun beat down on the landscape. Laurence walked and felt tired. He slowly glanced up at the sun. The bright light stunned Laurence, and he felt dizzy. Suddenly Laurence tumbled to the ground, completely collapsing on the road. Gonzalez and Coverton heard Laurence fall and looked back in a state of panic. Quickly they ran over to him.

"Laurence! Laurence!"

Laurence felt his eyes give out as the world fell into blackness.

Cody Thomas Chandler

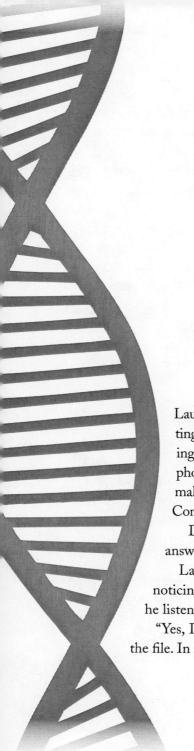

Twelve

Laurence awoke to find Dr. Conner sitting in a chair next to his computer, working readily on something important. The phone next to him rang. Laurence didn't make a noise or dare move to alert Dr. Conner that he was awake.

Dr. Conner picked up the phone and answered. "Hello?"

Laurence read the caller ID on the call, noticing it said, "General Anderson." Then he listened in on the conversation.

"Yes, I want you to tell him everything in the file. In fact, give the file to him." There was a pause as the general responded. "I don't care how he gets the information. You can beat it into him for all I care."

There was another pause while the doctor rubbed his eyes with his left hand and slowly exhaled.

"What do you think I pay you for? I didn't hire you to act like a US general so you could mess it up."

In return to that statement, the general said something that Laurence couldn't make out but it angered the doctor.

"Just make the damn announcement in fifteen minutes!"

With that, Dr. Conner threw the phone back on its hook and placed his head in his hands, mumbling to himself.

"Out of all the starving actors on the streets, I pick the dumbest one of them all."

He continued to gaze off into space until Coverton and Gonzalez came back through the doors to the room. Dr. Conner looked up and started a conversation with them.

"Why did he pass out? How much did he see?"

Gonzalez and Coverton looked at each other.

"We were just walking along, and then we heard a thud and there he was, lying on the ground. We had only made it to the first stop on the tour," responded Gonzalez.

"Good, good. At least this gave me a chance to give him the shot."

"What shot?"

The three men turned to look at Laurence, who was alive and kicking.

"Don't you two have something to do?" asked Dr. Conner, trying to get the men out of the room before they said something else that could jeopardize Dr. Conner's work.

Cody Thomas Chandler

Gonzalez and Coverton nodded and left through the set of metal doors.

"Listen, It's not important, Laurence. Nothing to worry about."

Dr. Conner smiled at Laurence. Laurence looked worried, but he trusted the doctor. It was probably nothing important, and even that couldn't suppress his underlying curiosity. He sat and watched the doctor type on his computer for a while before moving off the bed and pacing the room, lost in his own thought.

Within fifteen minutes, Coverton and Gonzalez had made their way back into the room. The men stood at the back of the room, stiff. Dr. Conner was scrambling through papers on his desk. Laurence was sitting on the cot, no longer feeling the need to pace the room, while looking around for something to capture his attention. A flat-screen television was conveniently placed on the wall. Suddenly it came to life with a flick, and a general appeared on the screen.

"Dr. Conner?"

Dr. Conner replied without turning to him, "Yes, sir?"

"Is it ready?"

"As far as I can tell."

The doctor winked, and the general seemed impressed with the good news. The general changed his line of vision to Laurence.

"Mr. Clark?" Laurence stared at the general. "I would like to see you in my office. I have some things I would like to discuss with you."

Laurence nodded as the television screen went black.

Dr. Conner stood and looked in his direction, as did the two other men. No one even made a move toward the door.

"So, are you all going to show me the way? Or do I have to make my own way through this place like a mouse in a maze?"

The men chuckled. Dr. Conner watched as Laurence left. The men opened the doors and led Laurence through them, Dr. Conner moving to the middle of the doors, looking out at Laurence. They walked on for a second before Dr. Conner called out to Laurence.

"Laurence, please be safe. You are the only one of your kind, you know?"

Laurence looked back and smirked at the doctor.

"I'll put it on my list of things to do, Doc."

Thirteen

The general sat behind a large desk, with a large window stationed directly behind him, sunlight pouring into the room.

"Please sit down, Laurence."

Laurence sat. Gonzalez and Coverton stood in the back of the room, in order to give everyone a sense of safety.

"Laurence, how old are you?"

Laurence thought for a moment trying to remember his own age.

"Ninety-seven, I think."

The general looked up at the man, thinking he was trying to trick him. Then he shook his head in confusion and went on.

"Laurence, hopefully you are aware that you are government property now." Laurence looked up at the man coldly, accepting his own fate. "And we are going to capitalize on your abilities for the continued safety of this country."

Laurence looked around as if his eyes were remarking sarcastically what his mouth didn't dare say.

"We need you to track down a woman. Her name is Sydney Wrathburn..." The man's voice trailed off, reading the files that he would soon turn over to Laurence.

"Currently, she is spending her time in Sydney, ironically enough, but only for a few days. You will go there and get to know her."

Laurence felt an irresistible urge of cockiness sweep over him.

"So what? Are you sending me there to spy on her? What has she been doing, selling drugs to kids on the street corner?"

Footsteps were heard making their way up to the front of room from the back. Apparently one of the men took offense to the words.

Suddenly a hand came down on the desk, clasping the file in its grasp. The files quickly came flying at Laurence as he put up his hands to protect himself. Gonzalez was infuriated by Laurence's words.

"You think this is some kind of game? Do you, kid?" The man reached out and grabbed Laurence's collar, pulling Laurence's face close to his own. "I have watched too many men die by the hands of the Wrathburns to sit back there and listen to you joke, you arrogant piece of—"

The general cut him off. "If you don't mind, we have important matters to cover here." The man loosened his grip and started to walk back to his position. "And if you ever do so much as try anything funny from this moment on, I will personally kill you."

The man walked back to his position, flames shooting from his eyes and mouth like that of an angry dragon. Laurence heard Coverton whisper to Gonzalez. Laurence then turned his attention to the file that was scattered across his lap. He looked carefully down at it, gathering all of the pieces of paper, until one caught his eye. The girl's photo was printed on it. Oh, was she beautiful too. Laurence could hardly look away from her long, black hair and green eyes. She was intoxicating, and he was already an addict.

"Her father, Anthony Wrathburn, is believed to be selling weapons to terrorists," the general started in.

"And the government doesn't want to take any risks. Your job is to get to know her, so you can find proof of these crimes, in turn, bringing down a growing terrorist cell in the Middle East."

Laurence skimmed through the folder, careful not to move too far away from the data files on Miss Sydney Wrathburn.

"What terrorist organization is it?"

The general looked calmly at Laurence, leaning forward and folding his hands.

"They call themselves Non'Masque. They bombed the USS *Assimilative* last year."

Laurence turned around to face the guard who had thrown the files at Laurence before. "You were there weren't you?"

The man grimaced as the general answered for him.

"Yes, Gonzalez did witness the bombing of the USS *Assimilative*. He was stationed there. Unfortunately, we believe that the terrorists now want more than the harm of a mere US vessel."

Laurence felt a wave of sorrow and excitement sweep through his body. He knew what he had to do for his country.

"When will I leave?"

"Right away."

Laurence nodded, and the general waved his hand for the men to take Laurence away. Before exiting, Laurence turned back and looked at the general.

"Oh, and General, I forgot to ask your name."

The general rose and looked at Laurence carefully.

"Abrams," he responded coldly.

With that, Laurence shook his head, remembering the name on the caller I.D. in the doctor's office and smiling at the lies these men were spoon-feeding him. If his mission wasn't so appealing, he wouldn't have turned to walk out the door with the two men.

Cody Thomas Chandler

Fourteen

The airplane soared above Australia, showing Sydney as dotted buildings. The plane only had a small amount of time left before it would land, and then Laurence would be off to the streets of Sydney, looking for a woman the government wanted.

The plane landed with a jump and slowly rolled to a complete stop. There were three of them on board the plane: Laurence, Coverton, and Andrews. Laurence would have preferred Gonzalez, but he was ordered to stay at the base, while Andrews took his place. They had been told that Andrews was a government official. However, remembering the previous events, Laurence doubted the validity of the fact.

Laurence impatiently waited to get off of the plane. He figured that these people had no connection with the government and had an alternative motive for sending him to such a place. However, Laurence felt this was a sort of vacation. He was required to become acquainted with a woman he didn't know—something the government would have prepped him for if they were behind this. Besides, if he didn't do what they wanted, what would they do? Shoot him? He was impervious to falling; Laurence figured bullets would be no different. He just relaxed and decided he'd enjoy his expense paid "working" vacation.

They walked through a tunnel to the airport itself, dragging their luggage behind them. Their walk led them through the masses of people. They made a turn around the airport walkway and found a barrage of doors awaiting their exit with lines of cabs outside awaiting passengers. Laurence quickly made his way with Coverton and Andrews through the huddled masses of people to the doors.

Outside, a cab sat several cars down, waiting to be plucked up and driven away. The driver waited until the three men had loaded their suitcases into the back of the yellow cab before asking them where they were headed.

"Etre Etonne Suites," replied Andrews coldly.

They all looked out the windows watching the beauty of the city unfold as they drove by.

The beauty of the surrounding area was so different

Cody Thomas Chandler

from what the men were used to that it seemed like a holiday. It wasn't long before they arrived at their destination.

After the man unloaded their bags, the cab sped away, leaving the men at the Etre Etonne Suites that overlooked the Pacific Ocean. It was a beautiful view, stunning perspective for a first time viewer. They had their suitcases as they walked in through the revolving door. Slowly, they walked up to the front desk and arranged for their room.

The elevator was located around a corner of a back hallway, and they reached it after Coverton paid the bill for their room. Upon opening the door of the hotel room, Laurence and the men found themselves in a large foyer that branched off to several bedrooms.

The three men stood in the foyer before retiring to each of their bedrooms. Andrews was the last man standing alone in the foyer. As they entered the room, Andrews mentioned he had been sent by the Pentagon to monitor Laurence since they had caught word of such a young looking ninety-seven-year-old man.

Andrews left for his own bedroom while Coverton resided on the two beds located in his room, watching the latest on the television.

Laurence, however, was in the bathroom, getting ready to go swimming in the pool they had at the hotel. As he looked at himself in the mirror, he noticed his six-pack of abdominal muscles, along with a toned chest and arms. He thought that it was most definitely the cure taking another side effect. But he was quick in his astonished viewing, because supposedly, the pool had a beautiful overview of the ocean and sunset at night, something Laurence didn't want to miss.

He came out of the bathroom with a swimming suit on. It, like the rest of the clothes in his suitcase, was dull and supplied by Dr. Conner's men. The other two men looked at each other, taking a break from their various activities to stare at Laurence.

"Where do you think you're going?" asked Andrews in a snobbish way.

"I'm going to the pool to take a swim. I'll be back in about an hour or so," replied Laurence, while grabbing a towel and key card from the corner table. With that, he walked out and allowed the door to click shut. He listened to the two men start chattering and arguing about him. It didn't bother Laurence. He knew that they were going to talk about him whether he liked it or not. He had a feeling that soon more people would be doing the same.

Laurence turned onto the flight of stairs, and for just the slightest moment, while he stood upon the first step, he thought he heard a canary in one of the surrounding rooms. He stopped and listened, trying to hear the sound once again, but it was gone. Laurence thought this was odd, but ignored the sound and figured he was just hearing things and continued down the stairs. He quickly made his way to the bottom, pausing and thinking about what his next move was going to be.

After turning a few corners, Laurence found his way outside to the local pool. Outside, he could see the red-orange sun setting beautifully into the rippling ocean.

There was no one else at the pool, except for a woman

Cody Thomas Chandler

who was in the corner of his vision. At first, Laurence paid no attention to her, trying to soak in the natural beauty of this place. But when he took another look, he was shocked into speechlessness. He couldn't tell what was more appealing, the sunset or the woman next to him. The woman also seemed to be caught in the same predicament, now admiring Laurence as he admired her. She had long, black hair that dangled past her shoulders, a very tan physique, and curves that made 1939 look like a Puritan colony. Her eyes glistened a clear sea green in the setting sun.

If he could have only known her thoughts, he would understand that it was no accident that they met. She broke the eye contact first, smiling and looking down into the water. Then she looked back up at Laurence, who had never taken his eyes off of her, and gave him a sort of wink to follow her into the water. And with that, she dove into the dull water, changing it to a sparkling diamond.

Laurence stood there for a second in pure shock at her beauty. She arose to the surface and pulled her glistening hair back with her hands, calling to Laurence with her body. She looked up at him, and he was still standing there, as if frozen in place.

"It's beautiful, isn't it?" she asked.

"Yes, yes she is," replied Laurence looking at her like a little boy looks at a super model on TV, before snapping out of it. The girl laughed a little and smiled, while Laurence looked away, embarrassed. "I'm sorry, what—oh, yes the sunset is very beautiful…" Laurence's voice trailed off.

The woman smiled, and Laurence's cheeks lit up bright red with his embarrassment. She went under the water, and Laurence put his towel down on a bright white chair next to him. Then he walked to the water's edge, watching as the water rolled off of the woman's body. She looked up at Laurence, who was still standing nervously at the side of the pool.

"I don't bite."

Laurence smiled at the woman's statement and looked away for a moment.

"Well I was hoping you didn't ... "

She giggled.

"Come on in. You'll like it in here—it's warm."

Laurence smiled again and walked cautiously into the pool, diving under before wading over to the woman. She looked at him with her sea green eyes, and her skin glistened. Her body called out to him again and again, and he listened. For the first time in his life, he felt love at first sight.

"So what's your name, lover boy?"

Laurence looked at her and then down, smiling to himself.

"They call me Laurence Clark, but the more important question here is, who am I so privileged to be swimming with?

She looked at the sky and smiled openly, revealing her perfectly straight, white teeth.

"I'm Sydney. And I am glad to have met you in Sydney," she giggled to herself. Laurence stood, wading in the water, looking deeply into her eyes while she did the same back at him. Finally she broke away, staring at the sun before she continued speaking. "If you don't mind, I should be getting out of the pool now." She paused, unsure of her next words. "The sun is setting fast, and I have other things to do. But maybe if we're lucky, we'll see each other again."

Laurence watched in amazement as Sydney slipped past him to the stairs of the pool and climbed out. She looked back at Laurence and smiled carefully. Laurence watched and wished she would stay. Finally, he decided to speak up as she was reaching for her towel.

"If you're not doing anything right now, would you like to grab a bite to eat?"

Sydney smiled.

Fifteen

The restaurant was barely still open when they arrived. It was a nice place on the coast, just a few minutes walk down from the hotel they were staying. It was a pure blue building, entitled *Vero's Amoreterno*, containing large windows outlined in white, overlooking the ocean.

There was no one else in the restaurant, except the bartender who was cleaning up from the night's meals and washing the night's glasses. He stood in a center bar that the rest of the restaurant revolved around. The pair walked curiously to a table by the windows, admiring the deep abyss of the ocean. The bartender walked over to the table and handed them two menus.

Laurence observed the menu with Sydney. Occasionally she would peep over the top of her menu to stare at Laurence, wondering what he was thinking. They sat there looking at the menu, making small-talk until their orders were taken. Then they sat for a moment before Sydney started a new conversation with Laurence. "So, Laurence, do you have a job? Or am I looking at a hobo?"

Laurence laughed at her joke, making her feel comfortable being next to him. But, for a second he hesitated. "Well, as a matter of fact, I work for the US Government."

"Really, and what do you do for the government? Kill people? Jump out of planes?" inquired Sydney.

Laurence chuckled again.

"No, not quite, I'm a tracker of sorts."

"And what do you track? Killers? Terrorists?"

Laurence liked her humor. She reminded him of himself before the cure.

"Hardly," replied Laurence, working to be secretive. "I mostly track shipments of important goods or the violations of treaties."

"Well, that would make you quite the knowledge base of laws, wouldn't it?"

"You could say that." Laurence decided now was as good a time as ever to crack another lame joke. "I prefer to think of myself as the Encyclopedia."

She laughed this time. "So, Mr. Encyclopedia, how would you describe your life?"

Laurence thought about it for a second before responding.

"Well, my life is mostly like a brochure. Lots of impressive things here and there, but nothing really interesting."

"Oh, Laurence, I'm sure you've done something interesting in your day. Tell me, are you on a case right now?"

Laurence looked around awkwardly, looking for an answer.

"Actually, I'm on vacation with two of my coworkers right now."

Laurence's voice trailed away as he looked out the dark windows. "Yeah, well, that's enough about me. Let's talk about you."

Sydney lit up again like a radiant ball of light. "What do you want to know?"

"What do you do for a living? Or am I the one that is looking at a hobo?"

Sydney laughed. "Well, I am actually a writer. And I like to travel…a lot, so I could be considered homeless, in a sense."

Laurence smiled at her, loving her sense of ingenuity.

"I don't think that if you're a writer that you can be considered homeless. Maybe a little crazy…" Laurence smiled. "But definitely not homeless."

The bartender walked up to the table and placed their food in front of them.

"Enjoy."

He walked away, leaving the two to eat.

Cody Thomas Chandler

Sixteen

Sydney released her hand from Laurence's grip and opened the door to her hotel room. Laurence followed under some other new, contagious instinct. As he walked in, Sydney closed the door, allowing the two of them to stand alone in the foyer of the room. For a moment, their eyes met, and they both were glad for the chance meeting at the pool.

As the couple made their way further into the hotel room, they knew this would be the start of something wonderful.

But as all good things start, they all too soon

end, and the couple's night turned into morning. As the sun began to pour into the room, Laurence awoke while Sydney was still sound asleep. Laurence figured it would be appropriate to check in with his roommates. Before leaving, Laurence left a note on the nightstand, telling Sydney he'd return in a little while.

Laurence carefully opened the door, stepping out into a velvet red hallway without a soul in sight. He strolled back from Sydney's room to his own all too soon.

Andrews and Coverton lay sprawled out on their beds; the TV was still on from the night before. On the table sat an open box of pizza, and the two men sported its sauce around their lips. Laurence headed straight toward the bathroom, closing the door behind him. Andrews jumped from the sound of the door, and suddenly he was awake.

"Where have you been?" asked the snobby voice.

Laurence walked grimly out to face Andrews.

"Just got caught up while talking to some people, and then I fell asleep at the pool, woke up this morning, and grabbed some breakfast. And now, by some ungodly stroke of luck, I'm here."

"Next time you decide to take a nap, how about you run it by me first, so I don't worry about you all night. If you die, I'm the one who has to take a pay cut."

Laurence looked cockily back into Andrews's eyes.

"I'm glad your worrying involves ordering pizza and falling asleep watching TV."

Laurence went to go back to the bathroom. Coverton

Cody Thomas Chandler

woke during the heated conversation and now sensed the tense air that was building in the room.

"Andrews, I'm going to get a coffee. Do you want anything?"

Andrews took his gaze from Laurence for a moment, allowing him to respond.

"No, I think I'll be all right."

Coverton moved off of the bed. He placed the shoes around his feet, tying both laces. He stood straight up and walked toward the door. An idea suddenly struck his mind.

"Laurence, why don't you come with me?"

"Sure."

The door closed sharply behind them, allowing for a blanket of silence from the ceiling to fall down upon them. Coverton took action and spoke first.

"So where were you really last night?"

Laurence looked back at Coverton, still reluctant to tell the truth.

"I told you already. I fell asleep at the pool, and I went out for breakfast this morning."

Coverton looked down, disgusted with Laurence's lies. They continued walking down the hallway until they reached the stairs, which they took fairly slow, until Coverton hit the last step and spoke once more.

"Well, the next time that you decide to fall asleep next at the pool, consider taking Andrews with you. If I lose you, it's just me and the proper government official."

Laurence grinned.

"I'll be sure to put it on my list of things to do."

"Good, hopefully you won't leave me alone again then?"

Laurence looked over at the wall clock, hovering above mountains of food at the breakfast bar.

"About that…" He trailed off. "I actually have to go grab something from the room. I'll catch up with you later."

And with that, Laurence turned and hurried away from the breakfast bar as Coverton poured himself a drink.

Laurence took the stairs back up to his floor; however, he passed his room and instead made his way to Sydney's. He knocked on the door, anxiously awaiting an angel to answer.

The door opened, and Laurence walked inside, not noticing the security cameras that watched his every move. However, even if he had taken notice of them, his vision couldn't have seen the extra person watching his every move from the security room of the hotel.

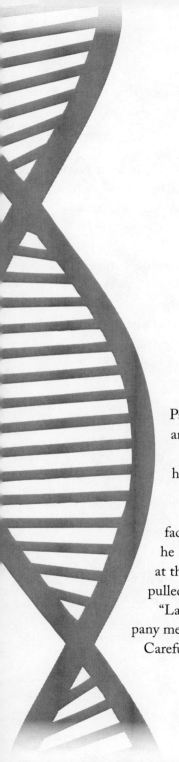

Seventeen

Passionately their eyes stayed locked in an intimate bond.

"I'm sorry." Laurence stumbled over his words. "I had to see you again."

Sydney smiled at him.

He reached out and held Sydney's face with his left hand, pulling it in until he kissed her rose lips. Their eyes closed at the first touch and opened slowly as he pulled back. She felt it and longed for more.

"Laurence, how would you like to accompany me to Florence?"

Carefully, he thought of the consequences

for his future actions. But he soon forgot about what he was expected to do, and just thought about what he wanted to do.

"When would we leave?

Laurence quickly put everything behind him, not caring about what Coverton and Andrews would have to say about him leaving. Besides, he had seventy plus years to catch up on and enjoy. Sydney responded quickly to his question.

"Tomorrow at noon."

Laurence looked at her and smiled carefully to himself.

"I would love to."

Sydney bit her lip and smiled happily.

"Good." Seductively, she paused. "Maybe if you're lucky, you can win my heart over again in Italy..."

"So I take it you don't like to stay in one spot for too long?"

Sydney giggled like a school girl.

"Oh, no. My father doesn't like to stay anywhere for more than a few days. Since my mother died several years ago, he has kept on the move, taking me with him."

Laurence watched her ever more carefully.

"Oh, I get it—you're kind of like a sightseer then?"

Sydney giggled again as Laurence grinned at his own remark.

"You could call it that."

Sydney looked at the table for a moment before picking up the key card to her room, slapping it carelessly into her hand repeatedly, thinking to herself.

"What do you say we explore the city before we have to leave this miraculous place?"

Cody Thomas Chandler

Laurence looked out the window to the town of Sydney and then back to his newfound Sydney.

"I think that sounds great."

The door slammed shut as the pair ran down the hallway, holding onto each other. Laurence noticed two men just coming up the stairs, each holding coffee. Immediately he recognized them as Coverton and Andrews. Coverton nudged Andrews to look at Laurence running by with Sydney, smiling and having the time of his life. Andrews noticed the couple, but then turned back to the coffee in his hands. Carefully as Laurence ran with Sydney, he split the two of them, and pushed Andrews just enough to cause his coffee to spill directly down his shirt.

Andrews's head snapped up as a reaction to Laurence's actions.

"Thanks!" he called out to Laurence, who just barely got the message before reaching the stairs. Quickly, he turned his head and smiled at Andrews before turning the corner and disappearing with Sydney onto another floor.

Eighteen

The airport was a busy commotion of sorts: people checking in, checking out, bagging in, and bagging out. And standing in the center of it all were Laurence and Sydney. They were hauling their luggage through the line; they had already passed through check in and bag in, now there was only carry-on luggage with them.

The previous day had gone by so quickly that Laurence had lost track of time. Day turned into night, and night faded back into day. During the couple's day in the city,

Coverton and Andrews had followed them around the city, noting their every move.

Laurence thought he had left Coverton and Andrews asleep in the hotel room, trying to keep them out of the loop. Sydney had called a cab, and they had left the hotel at ten a.m. They had taken a half an hour trip to the airport, spending another hour working their way up to this point.

"Oh, Laurence, I just know that you're going to love Florence. It's so beautiful there," stated Sydney while they waited in line to hand their tickets to the stewardess, who was checking people onto the plane.

"Well, it's pretty beautiful here too. I don't know if Florence has what it takes to beat Sydney in a beauty pageant."

They both smiled, and Sydney held onto him a little tighter. Laurence and Sydney were three people from the front now. However, there was someone who had been watching them go through the line, from yet another secret security booth, since they first entered the airport. And that person was now rushing through the lines of people to meet up with Laurence and Sydney in line.

"Your tickets please?" asked the stewardess as Laurence and Sydney both unhooked hands and reached for their tickets for the plane. Then simultaneously, they handed them over to the woman.

"Have a nice day," stated the stewardess with a smile. And with that, the two headed into the walkway extending to the plane.

Rushing from the back came Coverton trying to catch up. Coverton flashed his badge at the stewardess who immediately called security on him. She turned and tried to stop the man, yelling after him, as the gates to the tunnel closed.

Coverton shouted down the noisy tunnel after Laurence, calling out his name. Coverton knew there was little time to catch Laurence. He no longer had Andrews' excess flap holding him down anymore. Coverton had left Andrews in the hotel room in bed, dead from a spiked coffee. Coverton called out the beginning of Laurence's name, before another door shut the tunnel off from the plane completely. Coverton backed off the door. He figured he'd let Laurence have a little more time with his precious Sydney and catch the next flight to Florence.

Laurence heard the beginning of his name and turned around, searching for someone to be there, but found no one. Sydney noticed this and spoke to him.

"Come on, Laurence, don't want to miss our flight when we're so close, do we?"

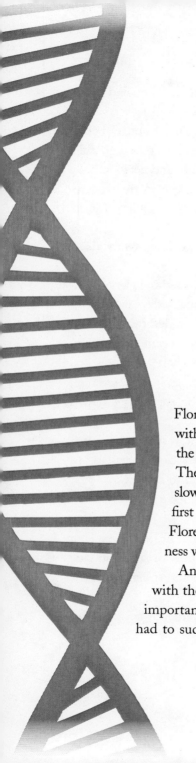

Nineteen

Florence was, in fact, quite beautiful with red-topped buildings rising above the slowly churning Mediterranean Sea. The water was a blue-green that washed slowly upon the sandy shores—the first attraction the two wished to see in Florence. However, their first line of business would be a meal with Sydney's father.

Anthony Wrathburn didn't come with them on the plane, because he had an important business meeting rescheduled and had to suddenly switch flights that morning.

Hence, Laurence and Sydney took their scheduled flight and would meet up with him at a later time.

Pushing their way through the airport and out into the world, they saw marvelous streets and buildings that once housed famous Renaissance artists and personalities. Laurence and Sydney were to take a cab to their destination. They would be staying in the Non'Chiaro Inn in Florence, a hotel in the heart of the city.

As soon as the cab dropped them off, the two walked casually up to the front desk.

"How may I help you today?" inquired the clerk.

"We need a room for—oh, how many days would you say?" Laurence asked Sydney.   "Oh, at least three days."

Sydney responded confidently and seemed to assure Laurence that they weren't going anywhere anytime soon.

"That will be five hundred dollars," recited the woman, as Laurence reached for his wallet, before being stopped by Sydney.

"Place it on the Wrathburn account, would you ma'am?"

The woman looked curiously back at Sydney as Laurence slowly retracted his wallet into his pocket.

"All right, but I'm going to have to see some identification."

Sydney dug through her purse. She withdrew her driver's license, and handed it to the woman. The lady inspected it for a moment before returning it to the woman and doing as she asked.

Soon thereafter, she reached underneath her desk and pulled out two keycards.

Cody Thomas Chandler

"Your room will be 335. Thank you, and enjoy your stay at the Non'Chiaro Inn."

The two smiled cautiously at the woman before rolling their luggage to the elevator and stepping in. Sydney pressed the button with the number three on it without hesitation, and it lit up, indicating its destination. The elevator tugged its way up to the third floor.

Laurence put his key card in the slot and opened the door, holding it open for Sydney. They walked inside and placed their luggage on the floor next to the beds before converging at the windowsill.

"So, Laurence, are you going to win my heart in Italy?"

Laurence looked at her with a loving grin.

"That all depends."

Sydney was quick to respond. "On what?"

"If you give me the chance to see the sights again."

Twenty

The two walked to the outside of their hotel, down a crowded street with amassed groups of people, each going their various ways. Laurence and Sydney, however, left the heart of commotion and walked down a brick sidewalk leading to a restaurant entitled Miss Deem's Ristorante, where they would meet Sydney's father for breakfast.

Laurence could only perceive what Wrathburn would be like, remembering the pictures he had seen of the man. Sydney still was unaware of Laurence's true involvement with the supposed US Government and their secretive operations against terrorism. However evil, Laurence felt that Wrathburn would be a slightly nicer gentleman, judging by his magnificent daughter.

Laurence was slightly nervous about meeting Wrathburn, considering why Laurence was supposed to be meeting with Wrathburn in the first place. Laurence no longer felt any need to focus on the mission at hand. His main focus was now placed on Sydney and leaving Coverton and Andrews behind to live a somewhat normal life.

As the couple walked, they held hands and pointed out the odd shaped buildings that lined the skylines of downtown. Together they giggled, laughed, and spoke calmly to one another. Their eyes moved from person to person and building to building, always stopping on the other. There was no doubt about their love at first sight, but no one knew how long it would continue.

They reached their point of destination, the secluded, backwater restaurant seated on Archer Avenue. They entered through the large wooden doors. There were dozens of tables inside, some to a room on the left, some to a room on the right, both separated by a bar in the center.

A waitress led them to the left side of the room and seated them. They sat down on the same side of the table, taking their hands off of each other to look at their menus, while awaiting the arrival of Wrathburn.

"Will I like your father?"

Sydney laughed a little at Laurence. "Of course you will. And I'm sure he'll like you too. In fact, I can promise you he will."

Suddenly, a man came up next to the table and began to take off his coat. Laurence didn't notice at first. But when he looked over the top of the menu he held, he noticed that he was looking at the infamous Wrathburn. Laurence stood up out of respect for the man and shook Wrathburn's hand.

"Hello, sir. I'm Laurence Clark. It's very nice to meet you."

The man exchanged glances with his daughter before responding to the gesture.

"Nice to meet you, Laurence. Now, please, take a seat. I would hate to keep these people waiting for our order."

With that, they sat back in the booth seat, Laurence next to Sydney and Wrathburn by himself. Slowly Wrathburn picked up his menu and began to scan it for anything that looked good. A waiter came up to the table, slipping out a notepad and taking their drink orders.

Wrathburn looked at Laurence, interrogating him with his eyes.

"Well, Laurence, what do you do for a living?"

Laurence hesitated for a moment before answering.

"I work for the US Government as a tracker." Laurence paused for a moment. "Mostly with treaties and laws for boats."

Wrathburn nodded as if he was impressed; however, the back of his mind was deep at work processing the probability of sitting across from a government official. Laurence was sitting across from the man, regretting his previous words.

"I see. What kind of treaties do you work with?"

Cody Thomas Chandler

Laurence thought quickly for an answer and settled on two acronyms he had heard in the airport from various groups of people. He just hoped they stood for something important. "Mainly UN or UNICEF approved treaties, sometimes I do smaller group treaties though."

Anthony nodded his head as if he trusted Laurence's statements. Then everything was quiet for a moment.

"I take it you two met in Sydney?" asked Anthony, staring at his silverware seated on the table. Sydney spoke up first, answering her father's question politely.

"Yeah. It was a stroke of luck too. We met two days before we had to leave."

Wrathburn smiled at his daughter's happiness. His mind churned out more possible explanations for Laurence's involvement with his daughter.

"Well, that's good."

The waiter walked back over to the table, setting the three drinks in front of the appropriate people and quickly taking their order.

And with that, the man walked back toward the front of the restaurant with the menus to put them away. The group continued to make small talk, laughing about jokes and learning more and more about each other. Wrathburn kept a keen eye on Laurence throughout the conversation and well into the meal.

The meal was lively and delicious, pleasing everyone's appetites. After the waiter took the plates away, Wrathburn looked at the pair for a moment before he spoke.

"If you'd excuse me, I have to make a phone call."

The two smiled a little. Sydney responded to her father.

"Of course, take your time."

Anthony smiled to himself.

"Why don't you two go check out some shops in the area?"

Sydney looked at Laurence, and they both signaled like it wasn't a bad idea.

"I'll be back in a bit, but you two should go enjoy yourselves."

The pair then made their way out into the city, while Wrathburn watched the pair leave before picking up the pay phone, pretending to make a phone call. Then as the couple walked out the doors, Coverton walked out of the restroom, whispering something to Wrathburn.

Cody Thomas Chandler

Twenty-One

The street was filled with little shops and outdoor sales. The two looked at each other and smiled at the great vastness of the city. To begin their search, they started off toward the closest shop across the street.

The shop contained clothes from foreign countries, along with a variety of souvenirs from the area that any standard tourist might want—exotic glasses and hats, postcards, and drinks. The two walked down an aisle of clothes looking for something that one of them might wear on a bad day.

"How do you like this one Laurence?"

Sydney was holding out a gray shirt that had Italian lettering and mimicked an American t-shirt. Laurence looked at the shirt and shook his head, not understanding what he was looking at. He was interrupted by a noise outside of the store.

Laurence turned to see a black car sitting in the street, with two men dressed in all black, sporting professional shades and earpieces. With a more careful inspection of the vehicle, Laurence could have read the license plate that said "WRATH 8" in a dull green lettering. The men were speaking to the owner of the store, who was sitting outside in the glistening sun. They seemed to be asking the man a question while he was nodding and pointed inside. Laurence took the hint.

"Sydney, we have to go."

Sydney turned to look at Laurence like he was crazy.

"What do you mean we have to go? We just got here."

Laurence hurried his words together.

"No time to explain. Just run!"

Sydney seemed to catch the hint, when the two men hurried toward her and Laurence. Sydney turned, and Laurence grabbed onto her hand as he quickly took the lead, running to the end of the aisle. From there, he led her through the fire exit of the store and out onto an alleyway.

They were running, the men not too far behind. The alleyway itself was about fifteen to twenty feet in width and paved in stones. Laurence and Sydney were running as fast as Sydney could go in flip-flops; the others were catching up quickly. Laurence knew that he could run faster, but he wasn't about to leave Sydney behind.

The alleyway was long, showing no end, but Laurence had to find an escape before the men caught up to them. He knew they stood no chance in a dead run against these men. Quickly, he turned himself and Sydney around a corner.

"Sydney run as fast as you can back to the hotel room. Don't turn back, and don't wait for me." Sydney hesitated on Laurence's words. "Go!"

With that Sydney took off running as fast as she could, ditching her flip-flops and withstanding the pain of hard cobblestone as she ran. Laurence picked up a board lying in the alleyway and waited. He held the board parallel to his face, over his left shoulder. Laurence knew the men wouldn't be long before they popped out around the corner.

With that he closed his eyes for a moment and listened. Their footsteps rang in his ears, clear as day. He heard the splash of the puddle from right around the corner. He was pressed hard up against the wall, fairly close to the corner. He opened his eyes and held his breath. Whoever these men were, they wanted something out of him or Sydney. Either way, he wasn't going to risk anyone finding out anything they didn't need to know about him.

The two men darted around the corner. With one swing, one man was unconscious on the ground with a broken nose. The board shattered in half. The other man was wearing a utility belt, much like Coverton's, that contained a knife. Laurence noticed this and used the knife to stab the man in the gut. Laurence hoped it was just enough to cripple the man.

Then Laurence walked over to the man who now lay fairly still from the knife, and leaned over him.

"Who sent you?"

The man went to speak, but blood poured out his mouth, choking him. Laurence looked at him sternly, then grabbed his collar and shook the man.

"Who sent you?"

The man stopped moving and lay still, dead. Laurence dropped the man. He stood up and rubbed his face from the stress.

In a matter of seconds, both men were either unconscious or dead, and Laurence was the last man standing. He was just outside a puddle of blood, making sure to move out of its way before it stained his clothes. He stopped for a moment, took in a deep breath, and let it go while closing his eyes. Then he walked down the alleyway headed toward the Non'Chiaro Inn.

Cody Thomas Chandler

Twenty-Two

The hotel room looked the same as it did when they first entered it. Laurence stood staring out at the city. Sydney stood next to him, tears slowly coming down her face. She held onto his arm, and he moved to enclose her to protect her from the men that were after them.

The city was now a shade of gray, coming down and engulfing the once incredible landscape of love and romance. Sirens from emergency vehicles could be heard below, signaling to Laurence the bodies had been found.

"Laurence, who were those people?" asked Sydney through her tears. Laurence looked at her and set her down on the bed.

"I don't know, but what I do know is that we have to leave, because whoever they are, apparently want us dead."

Sydney started crying harder.

"Who would want us dead?"

Sydney was apparently in a state of denial at this point, and there was nothing Laurence could do to stop it.

"Sydney." Sydney kept her head down. "Sydney look at me." Sydney looked up at Laurence with tears still streaming down her face. "Here's what we are going to do. All I need you to do is be strong now, okay?"

Sydney shook her head like she understood.

"Good. We are going to leave everything here, and go out through the back doors of the hotel. Then we are going to catch a cab to a train station and go into the heart of Europe. Once we're there, we'll catch a plane into the US. Do you think you can do that?"

Sydney shook her head and responded, "No... No, I need to see my father... he'll know what to do."

Laurence paused for a second collecting his thoughts and realizing how crazy he just sounded. Then he spoke slowly.

"Yeah, yeah. Let's go see your father."

Laurence gathered Sydney together and cautiously took her to the door. Slowly, he opened the door and peeked out. There was nothing to be seen in the hallway. Laurence pulled Sydney out into the hallway, tugging on her to follow him to the stairs. She was slightly less hysterical now, showing an effort to escape.

Cody Thomas Chandler

Laurence pushed open the staircase door and peeked around the corners. It was a concrete staircase with red bars wrapping around the center. He quietly pulled Sydney in and closed the door behind him, careful not to let it click and cause a disturbance in the silence. Laurence could feel the adrenalin running through his system; his body was completely alert, or so he thought.

They started down the first set of stairs to the ground level when they heard a click and masses of feet pounding concrete above them. Laurence looked at Sydney, who looked scared and in need of an escape from this predicament.

"Don't worry—everything will be okay, Sydney. I promise," Laurence said as he gripped her hand tighter as she half-smiled back at him. He led her down to the landing of the second story door. Laurence cautiously reached out for the handle, but as he did, his senses went off, and the door opened into his face.

Laurence was pushed halfway down a flight of stairs by the hit; Sydney was screaming at the sight. Through the door walked six men, all dressed exactly like the two men Laurence had taken out at the store.

"So, Mr. Clark—." The man who had opened the door into Laurence's now bleeding face walked over and grabbed Laurence by the scruff of his hair. Laurence felt the blood and was confused. What was happening to him? "You think it is okay to kill my people?"

Laurence couldn't answer, nor could he even see from the blood. Upon Laurence's inability to comply with the man's request, Laurence's head was slammed forward with a tremendous force against the hard, red, metal railing.

The railing cracked, and paint peeled off as he fell down to the next landing, his head bleeding on every step. Sydney was screaming, but now her yells were muffled by a hand clasped over her mouth. Laurence looked up at the ceiling, feeling his body go numb with the sensation that had overtaken him before. Laurence let out a sickly, blood-filled cough before his mind slipped in and out of consciousness.

Cody Thomas Chandler

Twenty-Three

Laurence awoke to find a tan sheet of cloth blowing in the wind above him. The room around him was a cloth tent. He had no clue where he was. He shifted his vision around and noticed he was on a cot surrounded by large, dull brown boxes. His head throbbed in pain from the blunt trauma.

He reached up and touched his forehead, finding a bandage wrapped around his bleeding head. His state of wonder persuaded him to sit up on his cot. He noticed that he was lying on another piece of cloth stretched between two metal poles. Laurence turned his vision to the right, trying to see what else lay around him.

There lying on the floor was Sydney. She was the same as she was normally—extraordinarily beautiful. However, she was bound to a pole supporting the center of the tent. Laurence stared at her for a moment before moving.

He stumbled slowly over to her, bending down and sitting next to her. He reached out with his right hand, touching her face. Her eyes fluttered ever so carefully.

"Sydney, are you there? Sydney?" Laurence asked. Her eyes fluttered and she awoke. Then she turned her eyes to Laurence.

"Oh, Laurence."

Her words were short and separated, but somehow lingered onward.

"Sydney, what happened? Where are we?"

Laurence was concerned for her; she looked sore and anguished.

"They took us … while you were unconscious … they took us … they took us … "

Her eyes fluttered faster and faster, causing a panic for the man who was now holding onto one of her bound hands.

"Desert … it's been … I thought they killed you … three days, Laurence. Three days."

With that, Sydney fell against the pole, unconscious but not dead yet. Laurence was, however, in a state of fear, never letting go of her hand, worrying what might happen if he did. Laurence let go in an attempt to find Sydney some food or water, to try and give her some sort of energy. He began to tear through the boxes, looking for anything he could give her. However, he was soon interrupted by a man dressed in plain robes and a turban. The man was apparently Arabian and carried a gun that was held to his body with a shoulder strap. He looked down at Laurence and yelled at him in a foreign language. Laurence looked strangely at the man, unable to comprehend anything the man said to him.

In order to punish Laurence for his ignorance, the man kicked Laurence hard in the side of his abdomen. Laurence responded by coughing, tasting a hint of blood accumulating in his mouth. Then the man reached down and grabbed Laurence by his ankle, pulling Laurence outside.

The world outside wasn't so much different from the one that Laurence had spent most of his natural and unnatural life around. There was blowing dust and mountains of sand in every direction. However, tents dotted the land, each like the one that Laurence had just been drug from. Outside a massed gathering of similar looking figures crowded around him.

Laurence watched as a black car drove near the cluster, having a license plate that read "WRATH 6." Then several men dressed in all black suits stepped out of the vehicle. Laurence turned his attention back to the group.

Once again, another man spoke out to Laurence, and once again, Laurence had no idea what the man said. The natives seemed to be getting hostile with Laurence; as soon as they sensed he wasn't going to move, they cocked their guns and aimed them in his direction. Laurence put up his hands as if to say he surrendered.

Then from the back of the group walked a single man.

Instead of a gun, he carried a crowbar and held it firmly in both hands. This man had his face covered by his turban, as did many of the others surrounding Laurence. His eyes were a dull green, offsetting the brown eyes of the other men. He spoke calmly, unlike the anger of the two previous voices

"Stand up."

Laurence did as he was commanded. The man walked around Laurence as he stood straight up, not daring to test the men.

"Mr. Clark, do you know what you are?"

Laurence looked confused as he watched the man twist around the circle of men.

"Well, do you, Mr. Clark?"

Laurence still stood there looking calmly onward toward the man.

"You are a plague of this race. You are not needed here." Laurence was perplexed by the man's statements. "That's why you're here, Laurence. So we can permanently fix you."

At the sound of his own name, Laurence no longer needed a face to put to the man with the crowbar. He knew who it was, and he was astonished. Laurence spoke as the man walked directly in front of his face.

"You already have Dr. Conner."

The man's eyes flared at the very thought of Laurence's ability to pick him out of a crowd. Without even a doubt in the man's mind, a crowbar came down suddenly and hit Laurence blindly across the face. It was a good blow but not enough to knock Laurence unconscious, as the metal staircase had. It did, however, slice down his face, causing a new wound to gush with blood.

"You should know that you're already dead then."

Laurence knew all this already and could even put together where he was and who these men were. He was somewhere in the Middle East, and these men were a part of Wrathburn's terrorist organization. Apparently there was more than one lie that Dr. Conner had fed him.

"And before I kill you for good, you will watch the death of hundreds of millions of people. To think, if you wouldn't have trusted me, then you would be the only one in all of the world who could stop us. But, now you are the worthless shell of humanity's failures."

Laurence sat awaiting the next hit. And so it came upon him from the very front, just as it had before. Dr. Conner took the crowbar and swung the dull rod into Laurence's stomach, causing him to churn blood from his mouth.

"What a waste you are. Purely pathetic."

Dr. Conner went to walk away before another surge of madness over came him, and he turned and kicked Laurence's face with the point of his left foot. Laurence flipped backward at the motion, landing squarely on his back.

"Sydney…"

Laurence's voice trailed off as he felt an extraordinary urge to go back to the pool and meet her again. However, Dr. Conner heard his pleas.

"Yes, maybe we should see what Sydney thinks," responded Dr. Conner as he walked into the tent that housed the anguished woman.

Twenty-Four

Laurence found the strength to finally open his eyes again, finding he was in another tent, his arms cuffed behind a pole. He could barely even stand to look around; everything appeared to be in a haze. However, through the haze he saw supplies on a table. His eyes flickered faster—no longer containing the strength to stay awake while the world swirled away into a darkness of night.

When he awoke, there was Dr. Conner working at the table he had seen before. Sydney was held to the ground by handcuffs that were held behind her back by a single chain that was attached to a stake embedded in the ground. Laurence directed his vision back to Dr. Conner, though everything turned from cloudy to dark and back again.

"Whatcha working on, Doc?" Laurence squeaked out at the doctor who was still busy working at his table.

"Oh, the cure, Laurence. Someone has to have its power when you're gone."

Laurence looked at him coldly, finally realizing he was just a piece of meat to this man.

"You know, just because we are in an uncivilized country doesn't mean you can't show a little respect and talk to my face."

Dr. Conner turned, looking sternly at Laurence, before walking over and bending down next to the man who was chained to the pole in the room once again.

"Do you want respect?" Dr. Conner raised his voice. "Do you want respect?" Dr. Conner was in a state of near screaming. Then he took Laurence by the hem of his shirt and pulled him away from the pole.

"You want respect? Because this is the only respect I show for pathetic things like you!"

Dr. Conner ended by punching him across the face, which was loud enough to wake the sleeping beauty on the cot, before throwing Laurence back against the pole. Then Dr. Conner went back to work at his table as Laurence swiveled his head around to look into Sydney's eyes. Somehow, they just weren't the same as they used to be—duller and less alive. But Laurence knew that he could change that once he got out of here—that is if he could even make it out of here.

The flap to the tent opened, and in walked a figure—a very, very familiar figure. It was a man, roughly six feet tall, and sporting the clothes of a businessman.

"Dr. Conner?" asked the man, and Dr. Conner immediately turned around to face him.

"Ah, Mr. Wrathburn! You must be here to check on my progress."

Dr. Conner walked over and stood next to Wrathburn. Sydney saw this and stood up, pulling the chain out to her father and Dr. Conner.

"Father!"

With a hardened hand, the man swung and struck his own daughter, throwing her back into Dr. Conner's work. She landed roughly upon the tabletop. Sydney turned and looked up at her father, tears coming down her face. Her arms were bound so that she couldn't rub the bruised area.

"You dirty little tramp! I raised you from birth, and this is how you repay me?"

Anthony was furious, his voice trailing off into the desert hills.

"What do you mean?" cried out Sydney.

"Him! You knew he was sent to spy on me!"

Sydney turned to look at her father, then to Laurence, questioning who was telling the truth.

"Father, I didn't know!" she cried out again, but he didn't want to hear her pleas.

"Whore!"

With that, Dr. Conner took control of the situation.

Cody Thomas Chandler

"Why don't we speak outside the tent for a moment, Mr. Wrathburn?"

And with that, Dr. Conner escorted Wrathburn outside, leaving the two alone. Sydney turned and faced Laurence, hurt.

"You were sent to spy on my father?" She nearly yelled at him, but it didn't quite come out right. Her voice was just too raspy to yell. "So, I take it the past week has just been a lie then?" She was still yelling at Laurence, though her mouth stopped moving.

"Sydney, they're lying to you ..."

Laurence's own voice trailed in and out due to his condition. His eyes began to flicker.

"I wasn't sent for him ... I was never ... kill your father."

With that, Laurence lost all hope of speaking, falling sideways down to the floor. Sydney rushed over to him and sat beside him for a moment, kneeling down near his head, realizing the feelings they felt were real.

"Look me in the eye and tell me you're not lying to me," she said calmly, staring into his deep, thoughtful eyes. Laurence lifted his head from the floor for just one more phrase.

"I'm not lying to you."

His voice made him sound nearly dead, and he collapsed back on the floor, watching as Sydney backed herself up to the table once again. His vision was playing tricks on him. Everything was rotating—the room spinning. Laurence was dying. There was nothing on earth or in heaven that could save Laurence at this point—the only hope was that of a miracle.

Laurence could barely make out the bits and pieces of the yelling that came from outside the tent between the two men. Dr. Conner was enraged at Wrathburn for reasons Laurence couldn't understand for the time being.

"I don't support your private organization for your men to interfere with my work," stated Dr. Conner.

"You sent him to spy on me?"

"I warned you that if you didn't fund my work I would send someone to investigate."

"So you send the master Sherlock Holmes himself?" said Wrathburn sarcastically.

"I saw something in him that no one else had, can you blame me?"

"Yes, yes I can, because what you saw in him is probably the same thing I saw in him during our breakfast together—ignorance."

"Somehow I doubt that, but think what you want."

"I will! Your research is almost as poor as your employees acting at this point."

"What can I say, the lack of funding caused me to hire some c-grade actors to try and play the parts."

"You sent him after my daughter didn't you?"

"What did you want me to do? I'm desperate for funding, and every time I try and get your attention, you look the other way. I can no longer continue to follow in my grandfather's footsteps and run this terrorist cell. It brings in less than your measly pay, yet I taught these men to defend you and respect you, just as they do me. Desperate times call for desperate measures, Anthony."

Wrathburn felt like he had just taken a slap to the face.

Cody Thomas Chandler

"So you want more funds? Fine! Find your own funds, because I'm not giving you a damn thing anymore." He paused. "And I'm leaving this camp immediately."

Dr. Conner then snarled, though Laurence couldn't see it, and returned to the tent, muttering, "You'll regret this."

Then Dr. Conner walked through the flap in the tent. He walked over to Sydney, who stood still by the table.

The man seemed enraged by his conversation with Wrathburn and hit her back down to the cot. Sydney was now bleeding and crying. Laurence couldn't take the scene of her suffering anymore.

"Leave her alone," he coughed out, while noticing her eyes light up like they had when she met him. Dr. Conner responded harshly.

"Don't worry—her father will be the first to die."

Twenty-Five

The needle had just slipped out of Laurence's arm. Immediately he felt the result of it, the cold spinal sensation, though this was not the desired result of Dr. Conner. Everything was still in its place—Sydney lying on the bed in the fetal position, and Laurence now sitting upward against the pole.

"See, Laurence, that wasn't so bad, was it? And to think, in just a short amount of time I'll have everything you would have had if it wasn't for me."

And at that, he went back to work, becoming greedier by the moment for the invincibility that Laurence only knew for a few short hours.

"As you already must know, you were given the reverse to the cure after you passed out in Arizona. And I must say, you've done everything as planned. You distracted Wrathburn long enough for me to recreate the cure from your blood. And as his interest was solely on you, I could get away with doing whatever I wanted without any interruptions. And I may finally be able to get away from this damned terrorist operation."

Laurence turned and looked upward at the man, while the doctor stayed busy at his work desk, not bothering to turn around. While the doctor's back was turned, Laurence's body was engulfed in a single swirling blue stripe. The only physical sign of the cure within a human— something Laurence hadn't seen in years.

"I'm a little confused, Doc. What exactly is this terrorist cell?"

"Well Laurence, to get the best understanding of how it all came to be, I'm going to have start at the beginning. Hope you don't mind hearing my life story. If you do, that's a shame and too bad."

Dr. Conner paused and cleared his throat. "When I was a young medical school graduate, I was looking for a job. Wrathburn was a growing businessman at the time and offered me a starting position in his corporation. Of course I accepted the position; after all, it was a steady income. After several years, I was offered a raise and accepted before I was given a contract. That was my fatal mistake. I was only informed of the freedoms of the job—

the ability to research and design whatever was within my ridiculous budget. However, I soon learned I had to oversee this cell of terrorists, designed to give Wrathburn the upper hand. And as long as I turned a profit over to Wrathburn, I would keep my job."

"When you say 'upper hand,' you mean … ?"

"I mean he used it to eliminate competition and make himself look like a philanthropist, funding the terrorists through a charity—which is of course a front. Then any profits that the terrorists made were given to bankers who laundered the money so it could be used by Wrathburn. In essence, it makes Wrathburn look like something he's not, something he's not even close to."

"So tell me. Why drag me into this mess?"

"To use the cure to make a group of willing, able-bodied men stronger. Then we could use these men to gain complete control over his industry at first, and then the world."

Dr. Conner paused, laughing a little to himself. "In fact, as we speak there are four missiles surrounding us that could be fired at any moment by Wrathburn. Think, he could gain control anytime he wanted, showing the world just who Anthony Wrathburn really is. But, as soon as he takes any action, I'll take care of Wrathburn, making me seem like the hero and assuring me power."

Laurence looked up at the man, nodding at his words, making it seem like everything Dr. Conner said was perfectly acceptable.

"That's all wonderful and all, but how'd you even know where to find me?"

"When I was a little boy, my grandfather told me sto-

Cody Thomas Chandler

ries of a man—yourself, who was invincible. I being a child at the time, was fascinated by this. However, I was dearly unsatisfied. Upon his death I inherited his journals, studying every page to find your exact location."

Then Dr. Conner took out another needle, and Laurence spoke out.

"Are you sure you want to do that, Doc? It didn't seem to work out so well for me in the end—in case you haven't noticed."

Dr. Conner blew off the remark and stuck himself in the arm. Then the liquid inside leaked into his veins, or so he thought. At once something sparked in his mind that something went wrong. However, in the world of Dr. Conner, that was highly improbable.

"Back to the story of my life now, if you don't mind." Dr. Conner twitched a little from the liquid. "Then with the knowledge of your location came the trouble of finding you. It took me several months to find the exact location of the old lab. Once I found it, I used my research checks to try and pay for the property from the government. However, they were stubborn at first and wouldn't sell the land to me. But with our economy being in the state it is, all I had to do was add a few more zeros onto the figure, and they graciously accepted. We started to build a shelter on top of the old lab and discovered the metal shaft and transporter that led straight to the lab. Imagine my surprise! And after several hard months of work, a mirage was finished that you fell for."

Dr. Conner twisted again, and this time, his arms and body crawled from the inside out. He knocked his work onto the ground, taking with him the needle that he injected himself with.

Curled on the ground, he mumbled to himself, "This isn't right ... something is wrong."

Laurence smiled at this and looked to Sydney before speaking back to the doctor.

"I told you that you didn't want the cure."

"What's ... what's wrong with me?"

The doctor was squirming on the floor, his blood literally burning. His insides were melting, particularly his brain and heart.

"Look at the bottle, Doc. Things aren't always what you think they are."

The reckless doctor looked at the vial and noticed something he hadn't taken note of before. Instead of being a plain label, the vial read: Hydrochloric Acid—12 Molar.

"Oh, no. No! No!"

The doctor cried out in the shear pain of it all.

"How? How did this ... how did this ... " His voice was disintegrating with his reasoning.

"Why don't you ask your laboratory assistant?" asked Laurence blandly as he looked toward Sydney. The doctor shook violently on the floor, until he collapsed from the rotting acid and died.

Laurence was in no mood to end up like the doctor. Quickly and mercilessly, he stretched the handcuffs that bound him and pulled the chain apart, gaining his freedom. The cuffs were still about his hands, but he could now move his arms freely.

Effortlessly, he took Sydney and pulled her up, taking

Cody Thomas Chandler

her in his arms and hugging her without regret. Turning her around, he grabbed her handcuffs and snapped them off too, allowing for her to move her arms with ease. "We're going to make it out of here, okay?"

She nodded in response to his question. He continued. "I promise I'll explain all this once we leave. But for now, I need you to be strong. Can you do that for me, Sydney?" he questioned, and she nodded, not ready to face the war that awaited them outside.

Twenty-Six

Quickly the pair shuffled through the boxes in the tent, finding one with uniforms. Laurence changed into it as Sydney, still in handcuffs, searched for weapons. She was unable to find any, however.

"Let's go!" said Laurence as he finished putting on the uniform. He led her out of the tent, pretending that she was a prisoner and he was a guard, taking her to a safe place, a place where they couldn't find her or hurt her until Laurence was finished with every last one of them. Walking through the groups of men, he led her to a truck and violently threw her in the back of a truck to make himself look like he was one of them. She lay still, knowing that he was going to save her from inevitable death.

With that, Laurence turned back around and reached down for a gun, but before his hand was even around the weapon, a cry was heard from the tent with Dr. Conner's body in it. The words were in Arabic, but Laurence knew that it wasn't anything good. Immediately after the words were uttered, every man in the camp cocked their weapon and aimed at Laurence.

At the very action, Laurence picked up the weapon lying next to him and aimed it back at the men. This action caused a fire fight to break out, bullets flying at Laurence and the truck that contained Sydney. He feared for her life, but had to fire back at the men. Laurence was rapidly firing back at the men, quickly eliminating a wave of them.

Before he could even attempt at killing the second wave of men, his clip was empty. Steadily, he ran up to another weapon that had been dropped by one of the men he had killed. As Laurence ran, he noticed that the bullets just glanced off of his skin, sort of like how when he fell, nothing was broken. The cure had taken a full effect on him again.

As he latched on to the other weapon, a rocket came sizzling at his face, exploding on impact, blowing Laurence back into the truck that held Sydney. Laurence crushed the side of the truck inwards and walked only a step forward before another rocket came for him. However, this rocket was aimed at the truck, and the engine seemed to be the main target.

Laurence turned away, and right before the rocket hit, he saw Sydney, her eyes gleaming hopefully up at him. But then, with thunderous applause, the truck burst into flames from the puncture of the rocket. Laurence was thrown backwards, while his eyes never left the back of the truck watching as Sydney was instantly engulfed by the explosion. Her last glance at him melted into his head forever.

He was upside down in the sand, still staring at the truck. His eyes couldn't even produce tears from the utter shock. But Laurence did what anyone who was in love would have done. He became infuriated with anger.

He rose up, taking nothing but his bare hands into battle. Nothing was going to stop him now; he was like the incredible hulk, and there was no Betty Ross to calm him down. He walked back toward the men; his face was calm while his eyes and body were seeking vengeance.

Another rocket was fired at him from the camp. This time Laurence watched it slowly come at him, then outstretching his left hand, he clamped onto the rocket and twisted around, throwing it back at the men. It exploded on contact, and this time, instead of killing innocents, it killed the very operation responsible for death.

Laurence watched the men scramble before being blown to smithereens by the rocket. He walked over to the few who survived and snapped their necks ferociously, like an untamed animal in the wild.

Then he spotted Wrathburn. Slowly Laurence walked up to the man, who seemed to be reaching for a remote that lay next to him on the ground.

"You killed your daughter," Laurence said angrily to

Cody Thomas Chandler

the man, who seemed to be more concerned with the remote than the deaths of his own family. To make him listen, Laurence kicked the remote out of his grasp, near a seemingly dead soldier.

"Laurence, what happened here ... it was all a mistake. I can make it up to you!" Wrathburn pled furiously for his soul. Laurence had no interest in his pleas. He reached down and took up the man's head in his hands.

"Laurence, please!" Wrathburn cried out for mercy. Laurence dropped the man's head. A shiny object in the sand caught Laurence's eye and gave him a new idea. He bent down and picked an ax out of the dirt. He held it in his hands for a moment before he heard sincere evil laughter behind him.

Laurence faced Wrathburn, who was looking at the supposedly dead soldier that Laurence had inadvertently kicked the remote to. The man pushed a button, and in seconds the sand began to shift. Beneath the sand were two large doors, pushing upwards, reveling a missile silo. Laurence was in awe, gazing out at the landscape, watching as more silos began to open.

The missile seemed to have less than a minute before it launched, and Laurence couldn't let it take off from the ground. He turned into a dead sprint for the missile silo. Then without even hesitating, he jumped down the chamber, digging the ax through the skin of the beast the entire way down, forming a giant gash.

The missile now seemed unusable, as sparks flew from the damaged electronics, and the chamber was quickly filling up with rocket fuel. Laurence had to escape; there was no time left for him to do anything else. He jumped higher than he ever had before and dug the tomahawk into the side of the beast again.

The side of the missile was probed by these hackings, helping Laurence make it to the top, with only seconds to spare. The rocket fuel was getting ready to be lit as Laurence ran away from the silo. As the ignition started, the entire chamber was filled with a fireball.

Laurence shielded his eyes from the explosion then turned to face the next silo. He took a deep breath and suddenly took off while Wrathburn called after him.

"You aren't just going to leave me here are you, Laurence?" He paused for a moment before he realized his fate was sealed beneath the jagged metal sheet that laid on top of him. "You can't stop them all!"

Laurence reached the next missile silo in a couple of minutes. Adrenalin was rapidly flowing through his already incredible body, keeping him on the edge. The silo was all but a mile away from his previous location.

Taking the ax as before, he sliced down the side of the missile, cutting several tubes at the bottom, allowing rocket fuel to leak all over the cylinder. Then he hacked his way up the side of the missile. However, the metal shell of the missile gripped the ax and wouldn't let it go. It was lodged several feet from the surface. Laurence knew he didn't have the time to take it out.

Instead, he climbed up the missile by grabbing wires in the gash he had already cut out. Then Laurence put

Cody Thomas Chandler

his feet on the ax handle, using it as a ledge from which he could jump to the surface. Laurence leaped and pulled himself onto the sandy surface.

The next silo was closer than the last, taking Laurence under a minute to reach. He stopped next to the silo wall, wondering how he was going to disarm the missile without an ax. Then suddenly an idea struck Laurence. He leaped to the bottom, landing on his feet like a cat. At the bottom of the chamber, Laurence grabbed several tubes attached to the missile and ripped them free of the machine. Then as the rocket fuel poured over him, he shimmied up the missile and the outer wall. Laurence reached the top and carefully climbed out. Then he stood up and looked down at the filling silo before he continued to the next silo.

However, there was little time left before the other missiles launched, meaning Laurence was pressed to make it to the final missile. He ran faster than before, realizing millions of lives were in his hands.

He heard explosions as the other two missiles went up in flames, but just ahead he could see a missile starting to poke its head out of its silo.

He was only a hundred feet away, and the missile was steadily rising from the chamber now. Laurence's legs should have given out from the strain, but he was running on adrenalin—nothing else had the power to keep him going.

From midair, he reached out and punched the missile's side with his hand. His hand tore through the metal, taking wires and fuel lines with it, while the metal took the skin from his hand.

Laurence fell smoothly into the sand, watching in horror as the missile rose hundreds of feet into the air. Tears fell from Laurence's eyes, not only from the pain in his hand—though it had already begun to repair itself—but from the thought of how he had just failed all the people whose lives were at stake, and Sydney.

With a stroke of sheer luck, the indent his hand had made severed the mechanics of the missile, and it stalled midair. Then he saw it come barreling back toward the earth, and immediately stood up. The missile came crashing down on a specific area, an area that was engulfed with the screams of a soon-to-be dead man. The same man that had doubted Laurence's ability to stop the missiles and the same man Laurence had left to die.

Cody Thomas Chandler

Twenty-Seven

Lonely, Laurence sat in the front seat of a cab, pondering the past week's events and the weeks to come. His change was now permanent, his life scarred forever. But on the brighter side of things, hundreds of thousands of people kept their lives, unaware of their near death experience.

He rented the cab in the backwater town of Terminus, located in Saudi Arabia. However, Laurence in his genius, put the entire fare for his trip to Paris, on a bill for the late Anthony Wrathburn. Before leaving the town, he phoned the US Embassy in France and scheduled a meeting there at Theatre National de Challiot, for the world's first glimpse at a new species of man. Laurence had to explain the situation at hand with a great deal of stress.

Laurence also asked for a committee to be formed to protect the cure and to keep Laurence asleep in the cryo-tube until he was needed. They were skeptical of Laurence; however, Laurence assured them that a blood test would confirm his statement. When they even doubted this, he asked them to call the Pentagon, and then they might believe their case. In order to try and disregard Laurence, they placed him on hold in order to call the Pentagon.

And Laurence waited...and waited. Finally, they responded. It turned out that Andrews was found dead in Australia, making a lot of heads turn in the US government. The Pentagon couldn't confirm Laurence's statement, but they were willing to send their best scientists to test Laurence's blood. Therefore, these people approved the meeting, but wouldn't approve the committee until the blood test confirmed these outlandish ideas.

As he rode in a cab, Laurence bent over, writing a speech on table napkins that the driver had stashed in the back of his cab. There were so many thoughts running through his head that he didn't even know what to put in or leave out. So he simply started with the basics.

But, the basics only lasted Laurence so long before he ran into a wall of intellectual horror. As they entered new countries, Laurence was forced to show the I.D. he was given to get into Australia. Every time he flashed it, the memories of Sydney came to his head, and he real-

Cody Thomas Chandler

ized what he had to do to make sure that the world never used this cure for anything ever again. If this cure was ever released, human life would cease to have meaning; no death would mean no motivation, determination, or the fear of never having enough time.

The theater at which he was speaking at the next night was a few blocks down from where the cabbie dropped him off if the maps of France he was given during the ride were correct. And those few blocks could be the most treacherous of his life.

The sidewalk was bleak without anyone to walk with. Laurence tried to keep it in, but it ate away at him, prying on his heart. His walk was slow and steadily paced, trying to get to the theater as soon as possible to prepare himself for the mess of a presentation that lay ahead of him.

Laurence noticed a man walking behind him but took no note of it, instead deciding to concentrate his energy on thinking. Suddenly, a gun was in the small of Laurence's back, the man that was walking behind him had snuck up close to Laurence.

"Pretend like nothing is happening. If you scream, I'll kill you instantly on the spot. Understand?"

Laurence shook his head in agreement, though he realized that he was invincible and nothing could kill him. The man cautiously led Laurence into a dark alleyway. They walked a good twenty feet into the alleyway before he stopped; Laurence likewise followed and halted his progress.

"So we meet again, Laurence."

Laurence recognized the voice, as he had Dr. Conner's. "Yes, yes we do."

The man took off his hood, exposing his face to the world.

"You killed them all. Now I'm the only one who can finish following Dr. Conner's procedure."

"No, Dr. Conner finished the procedure, he just couldn't read his own handwriting."

Coverton looked at Laurence with confusion. "What do you mean by that?"

"What? Didn't you find out already, Coverton?"

With that Coverton fired four shots into the chest of Laurence, though they all ricocheted off of him. At that, Laurence lunged forward punching Coverton in the chest. This threw Coverton back a good ten feet, while Laurence recovered his balance.

Coverton rose to his feet and picked up his gun. Slowly from his overcoat, Coverton pulled out an attachment and placed it on the end of his gun. Laurence was confused, but unconcerned.

"So you switched the vaccines? Two can play this game, Laurence. Just you know, I'm going to win."

Coverton then took his pistol and fired several shots at Laurence. The rounds were bright orange balls that seemed to pierce everything that they came into contact with. Laurence dodged them, and they shattered windows facing the alley. Then one ball hit Laurence square in the shoulder, and it threw him through the nearest wall of brick.

Coverton laughed his ability to crush such a powerful man. "Photon rounds," yelled Coverton, "Really quite a wonder how affective they are."

Cody Thomas Chandler

Laurence felt pain run through his body as he lay on the floor of a random building. Coverton had put his gun back in his coat and was pushing his way through the wall to Laurence. Laurence looked around in a daze.

Coverton reached down and grabbed Laurence by the throat, throwing him up against a wall, before punching him multiple times in the gut. Laurence felt the pain of the punches flow though him and wondered what this man had in store for him.

Then Coverton lifted Laurence onto his shoulders and swung him around, hitting his head off of various objects. Suddenly, Laurence felt himself move from the shoulders of the man onto a solid object in such a way that any normal man would have broken his back.

Laurence looked to the left and immediately heard a deafening buzz in his ear. His arm was sprawled out under a saw, and Coverton had the controls at his command. Laurence immediately tried to push against Coverton's dominating force, but could not. Instead Laurence braced his arm for the pain and squeezed his eyes shut. Coverton brought the saw down on Laurence's arm, only to watch the blade twist and spew sparks. Coverton stopped the blade, which had been sawed into a smooth circular surface by Laurence's arm. Laurence opened his eyes and looked at his arm in utter surprise—there had been no pain whatsoever. Then Laurence decided it was time to take advantage of Coverton while he was stunned.

With his right hand, Laurence reached into the man's coat and took the photon gun. Laurence pushed Coverton off of him, then stood up and rushed Coverton. He grabbed Coverton by the throat and ran him through the brick wall that separated the interior from the alley.

They came to a thud as Coverton rammed into a pole in the alleyway. Laurence beat the man with his fists, quickly bruising the man's abdomen and face. Then Laurence grabbed Coverton by his arm and threw him to the center of the alley. Coverton coughed up blood but somehow found the will to speak.

"Why, you no good son-of-a—!"

Coverton went to reach for his gun, but realized Laurence took it and instantly stopped.

"Are you looking for this?"

A man had appeared next to Coverton, holding an identical gun to his head. Coverton looked up at him in disbelief before the man fired a single shot right in between the eyes of Coverton.

Then the man took the gun and threw it onto the lifeless chest of Coverton, before walking over to Laurence, who was in a state of surprise.

"Are you okay, Laurence?" asked Gonzalez, while Laurence stared at him in complete confusion.

"Yeah, let's get the hell out of here."

Laurence paused for a moment, looking down at Coverton, and then shifted his gaze back up to Gonzalez.

"Don't worry. I'll take care of him once you are safely at the theater," stated Gonzalez. Then Gonzalez escorted Laurence to the end of the alleyway, turning back onto the main street before speaking.

"Now, if I'm not mistaken, aren't you supposed to be preparing a speech right now?"

Cody Thomas Chandler

Twenty-Eight

Laurence looked out into the crowd, rubbing his arm from where blood had been drawn to validate his case. He sat off the stage, looking down at his notes, waiting for an answer from the lab before speaking. Suddenly, a hand rested on his shoulder.

"Laurence," a calm voice said to him. Laurence looked up anxiously at a young woman who was apparently here to deliver the news.

"They came back with the results. Your

committee is being set up now," Laurence nodded as if he understood.

"Thank you." He whispered to the woman.

Laurence stood for a moment, pausing before he went out on stage. He had already been introduced by a Pentagon official. But the skepticism among the crowd had caused many attendees to leave before Laurence even spoke. Laurence was thinking about his next move as the theater anxiously awaited the night's new radical speaker. The downtown location of the theater allowed hundreds to attend with ease. The chairs these people sat in were black, creating a facade with which many disappeared into in their black tuxedos.

Suddenly from the side wing, a man walked up to the podium in front of the people. He was a white male, sporting short, black hair that complimented his tuxedo. Anyone could easily swear the man was in his early twenties, as everything on him seemed to be perfectly formed, without the sagging or wrinkling of old age. He arranged his notes for a moment before clearing his throat and speaking into the microphone.

"Hello," Laurence stated.

The crowd looked up at him and immediately understood it was time for them to be quiet, while Laurence fidgeted for a moment before continuing with his speech.

"To begin, I would like to welcome you all here tonight." He paused, building the tension among the masses. "And then I would like to ask how many of you believe in eternal life?"

A few people in the audience shook their heads signal-

Cody Thomas Chandler

ing yes and some signaled no. The man seemed one with the things around him.

"Maybe I should start with the basics, so I don't confuse any of you."

Laurence paused.

"My name is Laurence Clark, and I am ninety-seven years old."

The crowd gasped, and a few smirked at the thought of such a young man being so old.

"On the projector screen is my birth certificate." A piece of parchment showed on the projector screens hanging on either side of the stage. "And as you can all see, I am now, in fact, ninety-seven years old."

The crowd looked shocked at these numbers, some appalled.

"You can believe what you want, but there is an explanation for all of this, and that is the final cure."

The crowd stared at him in complete disbelief.

"In 1939, at the beginning of World War II, the government began experimenting with genetics that they had secretly seized from Germany. These became the work of a secret base in Arizona. This very base was built conveniently under my home town of Estosolo."

Laurence paused and looked up to the corner of the room for help.

"The scientists then released the cure into the water supplies there, killing everyone there except for me. I was then placed in a cryo-tube to ensure my survival when we were attacked. At the time, they did not know of my abilities or how the world would respond to this cure."

Laurence paused for a moment before continuing.

"A mere two weeks ago, I was revived."

Laurence felt a tear come to his eye from the thought of Sydney.

"However, the events of these weeks are irrelevant. I will tell you that I will probably never see any of you ever again."

Laurence paused and waited for a moment.

"I am here to tell you that I have powers that you cannot fathom and abilities which should have never been given to any man. I will go back into stasis, waiting for a time when my services are needed."

Laurence looked out among the masses, hoping for someone to close their mouth and pretend like they understood.

"But the details of my containment are complicated, far too complicated for myself to even understand. So I will leave you now with my good friend, Mr. Gonzalez, who will explain the rest to all of you."

And with that, Laurence took up his note cards and ripped them in half.

"Thank you."

Then he turned and walked off the stage, leaving a mixed crowd full of blank, open-mouthed stares and mutters of disbelieve.

Cody Thomas Chandler

Twenty-Nine

Laurence stood above the hole, waiting to be lowered down by the same metallic sphere that had taken him from the cryo-tube before. There was a group of eight men around him, all to verify what happened on the day that Laurence Clark went back into the cryo-tube. These men made up The Council. Everyone was an important leader of the Pentagon, CIA, or FBI; or they were very scholarly. There was only one man who was not apart of The Council that was there—that was Gonzalez. They all stood there waiting for the machine to accept their destination.

"Laurence, you don't have to do this if you don't want to. You can live with us. We'll find you a nice little bachelor pad," Gonzalez said.

"No, thanks. I'll take my chances in the tube," responded Laurence solidly. Then a call came out from another man that was working on the machine.

"Okay, men, she's ready. Form up!"

The group of seven men, which included Laurence, formed around the teleportation device. Then the man who was working on the machine pressed a button, and the sphere leaked into the center. It stood there just as it had before, staring at the men. Then, the sphere jutted outward and sucked all the men downward into the pit.

When they arrived at the bottom of the tunnel, the men all seemed to dry heave, but not a single one threw up. Laurence looked around, as did the other men, noticing the char burned walls in the dark abyss.

"Well, this place sure has changed a lot since we were last down here, right Laurence?" remarked Gonzalez sarcastically. Laurence just turned his head slowly to face Gonzalez, who quickly wiped the smile from his face.

"Well, it looks like I'm going back in through the hole. Wonderful," stated Laurence dryly as the other men followed him through. Soon enough, there were men scrambling away at the computers around Laurence again, just as there was before. Laurence placed the pads back on his body and attached them accordingly to the bed.

Gonzalez turned around and faced Laurence.

Cody Thomas Chandler

"I guess I was wrong about you, Laurence. You didn't turn out to be half bad." Gonzalez paused and reached out his right hand to shake Laurence's. Laurence put his hand in Gonzalez's. "And my offer on that bachelor pad still stands if you want to take it."

Laurence smiled and let go of Gonzalez's hand.

"I think this is the better way to go for both of us."

Gonzalez laughed and smiled at Laurence as he climbed into the chamber. Then one of the other men closed it, and Laurence sat still inside. He looked around and smiled to himself, wondering what he had gotten himself into. Looking over to another man, he watched as he typed in the process for the gas to rise in the chamber.

The pink gas arose from the bottom of the chamber around his feet and stinging his lungs and throat as it did before. But he sucked it in nonetheless, watching the men disappear from his view.

Blackness covered his vision and thought, but then just before he fell into a permanent sleep, he saw Sydney. She was running in a field of yellow and orange flowers. Her face wore a smile, and he could hear her calling out to him, "I'll wait for you, Laurence. I'll wait for you."

Postlude

The chamber slowly slid open, and the pink gas diffused through the air supply. Laurence flickered to life. He looked around to see a group of men dressed in suits of dirty white metal huddled around him. One of the men took off his helmet. The man was shorter, as were all the men, and had bleach blond hair with a very pale complexion.

"Laurence Clark?"

Laurence looked at him as if he understood.

"We were told to revive you in the case of emergency."

Laurence cracked his knuckles and stepped out of the chamber.

"What year is it?"

The men didn't hesitate in responding.

"We believe it's around 2067," stated one man calmly.

Laurence nodded in acceptance of the fact.

"What seems to be the problem?" Laurence asked curiously.

"Total war. We need your help to restore the peace."

Laurence listened intently to the man's words and then looked from man to man.

"So when do I get to start?" Laurence inquired of the man.

Then the man took a weapon from a holster on his back and threw it at Laurence. Laurence starred at it for a moment before picking it up. It was shaped like a shotgun.

"You can start immediately."

Laurence seemed intrigued by the weapon and the man's words and crawled through the hole. The men rounded up into a circle, and the same giant, spherical teleporter took them to the surface.

There was something different about the earth now. The skies were blackened, lightening flashed often, and the ground beneath was charred black. Laurence understood the masks and the metal now: this wasn't just a war—this was a complete annihilation.

He cocked the gun back and looked onward toward his enemy—an onslaught of mutants that roared through a human defense. Laurence looked around and as soon as he was adjusted to the black, a lightening strike occurred. In the light he watched as a falcon circled the dying creatures.

Laurence took his weapon and stormed off toward the front line, firing at anything that moved and wasn't dressed in a dirty white metal suit.

Cody Thomas Chandler